UNFORGETTABLE

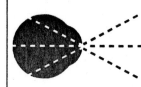

This Large Print Book carries the
Seal of Approval of N.A.V.H.

AN ANGEL RIDGE NOVEL, BOOK 5

UNFORGETTABLE

DEBORAH GRACE STALEY

THORNDIKE PRESS
A part of Gale, Cengage Learning

GALE
CENGAGE Learning·

Detroit • New York • San Francisco • New Haven, Conn • Waterville, Maine • London

GALE
CENGAGE Learning

LIBRARY OF CONGRESS CATALOGING-IN-PUBLICATION DATA

Staley, Deborah Grace.
    Unforgettable / by Deborah Grace Staley. — Large Print edition.
        pages cm. - (An angel ridge novel series #5) (Thorndike Press Large Print Clean Reads)
    ISBN-13: 978-1-4104-5545-1 (hardcover)
    ISBN-10: 1-4104-5545-9 (hardcover)
    1. Life change events—Fiction. 2. Mayors—Tennessee—Fiction. 3. Homecoming—Fiction. 4. Tennessee—Fiction. 5. Large type books. I. Title.
PS3619.T348U54 2013
813'.6—dc23   2012045028

Published in 2013 by arrangement with BelleBooks, Inc.

Printed in Mexico
2 3 4 5 6 7 17 16 15 14 13

For Becky Guyton

*Proofreader extraordinaire,
wonderful cheerleader, sounding
board, steadfast friend.*

A READER'S NOTE
FROM DIXIE

(Spoiler alert! You may not want to read
this if you have not read the other
Angel Ridge Novels.)

Hey, y'all. Dixie Ferguson here. Welcome to
Angel Ridge! Boy, it's been a while since
we've had a visit. But don't worry. I'll get
you caught up on all our news.

If you've been following along, you'll
know that a little more than six years ago,
Candi Heart moved to Angel Ridge and
snagged our sheriff, Grady Wallace. Beings
as she was young and from the mountains,
she wanted a long courtship. Long story
short, they're finally about to get married
just a few months from now, in June. That
Grady sure is a patient man.

And then Jenny Thompson fell into
trouble and lost her newspaper business to
the thugs that followed poor little Candi to
town. Needless to say, Jenny's not with us

7

anymore. Whether or not she died in that explosion, well, I could tell you, but then I'd have to kill you because that information is classified.

A year and a half later, Josie Allen moved back to Angel Ridge after finishing up her studies in library science. She took over our library and snagged the heart of Cole Craig, who'd had his eye on Josie since they were in middle school. Boy, did some fireworks fly between those two.

And last, but certainly not least, my big brother, well one of them, Blake Ferguson, set his sights on the new lady doctor in town, Janice Thornton. Her long lost uncle, Doc Prescott, had been our town doctor for better than forty years. With him ready to retire, it seemed natural that she fill the job, her being family and all. Turns out, she'd been looking for a home her whole life. You know, a place to belong? And she found it, right here with my brother.

So, now more than four years have passed. The town's changed a lot. Times have been hard, and some of our town residents have had to move on. But we are so happy that you've chosen to visit us again. We sure are glad to see you.

DIXIE'S WELCOME

Ah, Spring in East Tennessee. I love watching all the tulips, azaleas and dogwoods bloom. There's just something hopeful and uplifting about seeing such a riot of color after the gray of winter, don't you think? When the earth is reborn after its slumber and the temperatures warm, why you can practically feel change in the air. And trust me, in Angel Ridge change for some is a good thing, for others, not so much. In fact, some folks around here can dig in their heels and cause the ones wanting to make the changes a heap of trouble.

But first, let me tell you a little about the town we call home. Angel Ridge, population three hundred forty-something. Sorry, I've lost count, what with all the comings and goings of late. The town's located in the valley of the Little Tennessee River and was established in 1785. In the early days, its first families — the McKays, the Wallaces, the Houstons, the Joneses, and the Craigs — staked their claims on hundreds of acres of the richest bottomland anyone had ever seen. They built big ol' homes near the meandering river and operated prosperous plantations. Well, all except for the Craigs. They were traders and craftsmen. Men of commerce, as it were. Meanwhile, the town developed above the river on a high ridge.

In the early 1970s, the Flood Control Board came in and bought up most of the property along the flood prone river, and those stately homes that some called relics of a bygone era, were inundated in the name of progress. But those who built more modest Victorians near town up on the ridge? Well, their homes are still standin'. Of course, the families who lost theirs to the newly formed Tellassee Lake moved up to the ridge as well and built elaborate Victorian mansions such as this quaint little town had never seen.

Most of the families I mentioned earlier are still around. These are hardy folks. Why, in all the time they've lived here, they've endured Indian attacks, floods, divided loyalties in the Civil War, and yes, even feuds. The older folks are still marked by the hardships of the past, but the young

10

people of the town hope to move beyond old hurts to create a new generation made strong because of their roots.

For the last six or so years, Angel Ridge has seen a lot of change. You see, the economy here and everywhere else has taken a bad turn that has resulted in a number of businesses and their owners pulling up stakes and moving out. Unfortunately, most of the buildings on one side of Main Street have stood empty for some time now.

Then a little lady named Candi Heart (I know, don't that name just beat all?) came to town and turned convention on its ear by opening up a girly shop called Heart's Desire right across the street from the McKay Bank & Trust Company. Let me tell you, her "nice" and "naughty" window displays just about give our town matriarch, Harriet McKay, a heart attack every time she walks out the front door of her bank. But that doesn't seem to bother Candi much. Her business has been going strong for years now. Yep, that girl's a force to be reckoned with. She's not lettin' anything stop her. You gotta love girl power.

Speaking of which, that explosion at the newspaper was something of a wake-up call for Frannie Thompson. Her sister, Jenny

Thompson, ran that newspaper and was *allegedly* killed in the explosion. Conspiracy theorists, including myself, aren't so sure. Nevertheless, after the tragic loss of her sister, Frannie decided to make some life changes that included working out a plan, directly tied to Angel Ridge, that will fill all those empty buildings on Main.

Standing right square in her path is not only Harriet McKay, but also some of the older town folk. Complicating matters is our mayor, Patrick Houston. My dear best friend and his wife, Susan, lost her brave battle with cancer a few years back. Ever since she passed, and for that matter, even before, he's been a different person. Someone I haven't been proud to say I've known most of my life. There was a time when we were all the best of friends: me, Susan, Patrick, my brother, Blake, Grady Wallace, Cole Craig, and Jonathan Temple. But the fact is, after Patrick married Susan, he changed, and we never got along, despite the fact that I made quite the herculean effort.

Well, that's all I can say about that without gettin' riled up, and I'm determined to make a good impression. So, while you're here visiting with us, be sure to come by my diner, Ferguson's. Tonight's special is spaghetti with meat sauce, garlic bread, and sweet iced tea, of course. Also, I've got a new recipe for tiramisu I'll be trying out to give the place a cosmopolitan feel. Don't that just make your mouth water?

So, enjoy your visit, and I'll count on seeing you a bit later.

CHAPTER 1

Everyone in Angel Ridge thought Frannie Thompson's sister was dead. For all practical purposes, she was.

Frannie shifted her briefcase and purse to her other hand to open the heavy glass and wooden door to the courthouse. After checking the directory, she took a long stairway to the second floor.

Her sister, Jenny Thompson, had been forced to enter witness protection after uncovering the South's version of the mob with remnants in Angel Ridge. Everyone in town assumed Jenny had died in an explosion that leveled her newspaper offices, but Frannie and a few others knew the truth. Still, with their contact limited to correspondence exchanged secretly through the authorities, Frannie would never see her older sister again.

At the top of the stairs, she wound her way through a labyrinth of hallways until she found the mayor's office. Taking a deep breath, she smoothed her skirt and hair, then opened the door.

A young woman, sitting behind a desk in the lobby, looked up as Frannie entered. "May I help you?"

Frannie smiled. "Yes. I have an appointment with the mayor at nine."

The woman looked at her computer. "Frannie Thompson?"

"Yes."

She nodded. "I'll, *um,* let him know you're here. If you'll just have a seat."

"Thank you."

Frannie sat, but found it odd that the receptionist didn't go to the mayor's office or call him. Instead, she seemed to be texting someone. Frannie checked her watch. Ten minutes before the hour.

"Can I get you a cup of coffee?"

There was no, *He'll be with you in a moment.* Interesting.

"No, thank you."

The woman just smiled and turned her attention to her computer, typing at a furious speed.

Frannie pulled a file from her briefcase that contained her construction plans, approved by the Building Commission, for the project she intended to implement in town.

The change of use signs had been up for several weeks on the buildings on Main Street she would be purchasing from Bud DeFoe. She just needed the Council's approval on a couple of details to give her a green light, and she'd be in business. Just a small formality, and her dream would become a reality.

Twenty minutes ticked by. She looked up when she heard a commotion at the back of the office: a door closing, someone grumbling, another door closing. Frannie shot a questioning look at the receptionist who didn't meet her gaze.

The intercom beeped, and the receptionist picked up the handset, then replaced it.

"Ms. Thompson? The mayor will see you now. If you'll follow me?"

Frannie stood, and the forgotten folder on her lap slid to the floor. Papers scattered across the carpet. Frannie bit back a curse, then tried to quickly gather and put the papers back in order.

The receptionist came over to lend a hand. "Thank you," Frannie murmured, embarrassed. Not the impression of the slick, professional she'd intended to project today.

"Karen!" a deep voice bellowed. "What's going on? Did she leave?"

"Coming," Karen said.

The mayor's grumbling followed him back into his office.

"I'm sorry," Karen said.

"Is he always this cheerful?" Frannie joked.

The woman just smiled as she handed Frannie the last of the papers. Frannie shoved it all back into the folder and followed Karen to the mayor's office. She didn't need the man cheerful. She just needed a spot on the agenda of the upcoming meeting of the Town Council. On previous visits to Angel Ridge, she'd tried to meet with the mayor and bring him along on her plan, but he was never in. She hadn't worried too much about it because she'd been assured by her architect and contractor, Cole Craig and Blake Ferguson, that the mayor would welcome her project to help revitalize downtown.

Karen knocked on an open door, then entered. "Mayor, this is Ms. Thompson."

Frannie took a few steps into the office. The man had his back to them, typing something on a computer keyboard at the credenza behind his desk. She'd expected an older man with gray hair, but he had the dark hair of someone much younger.

"Yes, yes. Come in and have a seat," he

mumbled.

Karen smiled apologetically and retreated.

Frannie stepped into the room, but didn't sit. She waited for the man to face her. When he didn't, she said, "Should we re-schedule?"

His sigh was audible. He swiveled his high-backed leather chair to face her.

Frannie took a step back. "You . . ." She found herself face-to-face with the man she'd shared an anonymous make-out session with in the middle of a blizzard that awful winter she'd lost her sister. In the years since that night, she'd done her best to forget. It had been just a kiss, after all, but her body had betrayed her, and the memory of it wouldn't fade. What they'd shared that night had gone beyond a simple kiss. God, how she'd prayed she would never see him again.

The mayor stood and walked around his desk. When he was close enough to touch, he extended his hand and said, "Patrick Houston. I'm the mayor of Angel Ridge."

Patrick. The mayor's name was Patrick. Frannie didn't take his hand. Didn't speak. Just looked into those haunted, gray eyes she remembered so well. She also remem-bered having the devil of a hangover the day after. Learning the truth about him had only made it worse.

Finally, she found her voice. "You're the mayor."

He rested his hands on his hips and tried to look anywhere but at her, indicating he just might feel remorse. "Yes. Won't you sit?" he said, waving a hand toward the chairs situated in front of his desk.

She did, heavily, and tried to keep her mouth closed as he leaned against the front edge of his desk, facing her. Only inches separated them, and her treacherous body reacted to an attraction she wished she didn't feel.

He cleared his throat. "What can I do for you, Ms. Thompson?"

"Did you consider skipping our meeting because you wanted to avoid seeing me? Is that why you were late?" she ground out, anger displacing the shock.

"I'm afraid I didn't look at my schedule at all, so I wasn't aware that I had an appointment."

Was he actually going to pretend he didn't know her?

"What can I do for you, Ms. Thompson?" he repeated.

Frannie looked at the file resting on top of the briefcase in her lap. Unbelievable.

"Ms. Thompson?"

He was in for a shock if he thought she would play along to make this more comfortable for him. "I had no idea you were the mayor. Your first name isn't on any of the information I've seen. Just your initials."

He absently rubbed his chin, which made her notice he hadn't bothered to shave. "Yes, well, the only thing anyone around here cares about is that my last name is 'Houston.'" He actually smiled then and added, "A Houston has been the mayor of Angel Ridge for more than a hundred years."

"How nice for you." Anyone else might have found that smile charming, but not her. She stood. "However, it's your *first* name that would have mattered to me, since that was all you cared to share. It would have also been nice if you'd included that you're married."

He pushed away from his desk, standing straighter. A frown pulled at his brow. Dear Lord, in the light of day he was too handsome for words. Dark wavy hair, brushed back from his face and spilled over the collar of his casual polo-style shirt. There must be any number of women who wouldn't care that he was married. She, however, was not one of them.

"I don't understand."

"No? Neither did I."

She took a long step forward that brought her to stand squarely in front of him. The palm of her hand itched with the desire to slap him. A lot of years had passed since that night, and the rush of emotion she felt surprised her. But no woman liked to be played the fool. Frannie was no exception.

She tossed the folder containing her plans onto his desk. "I'd like to submit that at the next meeting of the Town Council. If you have questions, you can call my architect."

Turning, she strode from the office.

As she stepped out of the courthouse into the bright morning sunshine, Frannie slid oversized dark glasses onto her nose. She walked briskly across Town Square to a park bench near the tall, bronze angel monument standing sentinel on a brick pedestal. She sat, dropping her purse and briefcase onto the damp grass.

Anger roiled up inside her, teasing the edges of a full-on anxiety attack. She took a deep breath, in through her nose, out through her mouth on a slow eight count — just like the therapist had taught her. She gave up after losing track of how many times she'd repeated the technique. Her anger still simmered, but the panic had subsided.

She'd been in and out of town now for

months and hadn't once run into the man she'd met in the bar that night. It had been a full-on blizzard and just after her sister had gone underground. They must have been the only two people crazy enough to venture out in the weather, because it had just been the two of them there. He'd been drunk, and she'd been three whiskeys on the way there. His kiss, like the liquor, was a distraction from the pain of losing her sister. But in the sobering, bright light of the next day, she'd run into him at the town diner. Not only had she learned that he was married, but also that his wife had just been diagnosed with cancer.

She closed her eyes. Big mistake. The memory was there, raw and vivid, as if it had just happened.

That night Frannie had to swipe at the tears as she drove the icy roads. Visibility had been bad enough without her blubbering. Staying at Jenny's house, instead of feeling comforted, she'd felt closed in by her things, claustrophobic. She'd missed Jenny so much, and Frannie just wanted her sister back. How could Frannie go through life knowing Jenny was out there somewhere all alone?

Ahead, a sign glowed in the darkness through the snow. Frannie slowed and pulled over. Jimmy's Bar. Perfect. She could use a drink. In fact, getting smashed held great appeal at the moment. Anything to not feel for a while.

The windowless metal door swung inward. The interior was dark and sparsely populated, which suited her fine. She sat at the bar.

A thin man with a face that said it had seen more than he'd care to recount asked, "What'll you have?"

"Jack and Coke."

The man turned away to get her drink.

Frannie put her purse on the bar, and the folder the lawyer had given her slid out. The words "Last Will and Testament of Violet Jennings Thompson" glared at her. What a lie she was living. When the man had heard she was in town, he'd hiked through the snow to Jenny's house to bring it to her, instructing her on the probate process she wouldn't be able to begin. Another thing she'd have to discuss with the sheriff when the weather cleared. How was she supposed to deal with all this when she was still grieving for her sister?

She shoved the file back into her bag and shrugged out of her coat. Before she could unwind the long, green scarf her sister had gotten Frannie for her birthday, the last birthday they'd ever spend together, the man returned with her drink then went back to watching the basketball game on the television that sat in the corner of the long, narrow room. No conversation. That suited her, too.

She tossed the dark straw on the wooden bar and disposed of half the beverage in one long swallow. A man sitting four stools down from her watched. She didn't much care; let him look. The initial burn of the whiskey spread a delicious warmth through her chest and lower. She downed the rest, and her fingertips started to tingle. She set the heavy tumbler down with a satisfying thud.

"Another." Screw the niceties. Her sister had been taken from her. There was no room for nice in her world.

The man took the glass and made her another drink.

The other lone customer was still looking at her, so she looked back intending to say, "What?" but when she met his gaze, she stopped short. From the glassy look in his clear gray eyes, she'd say he'd had a few himself. He lifted his glass, took a drink, and hunkered down, forearms on the bar, his focus returned to the liquid in his glass.

At some point during the silent exchange, the bartender had brought her drink —

minus the straw — and disappeared. He'd also left a bowl of pretzels. Her gaze swung back to the man with the empty eyes, but he'd obviously forgotten about her and returned to his own personal hell. She wondered what was going on at home that prevented him from getting drunk there. Maybe he was from out of town like her. She chuckled and took another drink. She couldn't imagine why anyone would be traveling the back roads of East Tennessee in a blizzard.

He shifted his gaze to hers.

She looked back. He was handsome, in a disheveled, dark-whiskered, shaggy-hair-that-needed-a-trim sort of way. It fell in waves around his face. He shoved a hand into the mass and pushed it back toward his crown, then stood, stumbled and found his balance before moving her way. She turned away and took another long draw on her drink, not sure she wanted company, but nevertheless intrigued by the dark stranger whose high-end, designer clothing said he didn't fit in a dive like this. She chuckled again. She supposed she looked like she didn't fit either, but the selection of bars in the heart of the Bible belt was not wide or varied.

He sat next to her without asking her

26

permission. His empty glass had been abandoned at his previous spot at the bar. The bartender set another in front of him without asking, making Frannie reassess. The guy must be a regular.

He swallowed half his drink, set the tumbler down and said, "What brings you to a place like this in a snowstorm?"

Frannie took a drink as well. Her whole body was warm now. "I could ask you the same question."

"If you were from around here, you'd know." He had another sip of his drink and turned back to her. He took his time looking at her. "You don't belong here."

Emboldened by the whiskey, she looked her fill of him as well. The warmth radiating to the rest of her body from her midsection shifted lower. "Where do I belong?"

They were sitting close, too close, but she noted the fact too late.

"Is this a guessing game, then?"

"I don't play games."

"Everybody plays. Not everyone wins." He swallowed the rest of his drink. "What's your name?"

She considered for a moment, then said, "Frannie."

"I'm Patrick."

He held out his hand and she stared at it,

then twenty-seven years of breeding kicked in, and she offered hers. His fingers were warm and well-shaped. This wasn't a man who worked with his hands. He was a professional of some sort. Maybe he was a lawyer, too. He had that air about him, like he'd stripped off a jacket and tie and left them in an expensive car before coming into the bar.

"You have nice hands," he said, still holding hers. He brushed his thumb across the ring she wore. Her college ring. She didn't miss his glance at her other hand to see if she wore a diamond or wedding band. "What brings you here, Frannie?" he asked, his thumb now moving back and forth across her knuckles.

Her hand felt good in his; human contact felt good after so much loss and emptiness, so she traced the lines of his palm with her fingertips. "I needed a drink."

He chuckled. "I think you had two, not that I'm counting."

She smiled. "And I'm still not drunk, so I think I need another."

He glanced toward the bartender and lifted his chin, taking care of her request. She brought the drink to her lips and downed it in one swallow. She resisted the urge to cough and ruin the effect.

"Impressive," he noted with a raised eyebrow. "Better?"

She smiled, but her hair fell like a curtain, separating them. He pushed it back, leaving her face and neck exposed and vulnerable. He leaned in, his bourbon-laced breath warm on her cheek, his dark stubble not unpleasantly rough against her cheek. He sighed and nudged her ear with his nose; his warm lips caressed the lobe.

She should move away, but the whiskey and the sadness pressing on her soul interfered with her ability to act like the proper young lady her mother had raised her to be.

"Tell me to stop," he whispered, but pressed another kiss to the vulnerable spot behind her ear. He put his arm along the bar in front of her and slid the back of his fingers along her jaw until their gazes locked again.

Raw pain had flowed between them. They'd both wanted to feel something else — needed to feel anything else. So she'd leaned in and tasted his lips.

Frannie ripped her glasses off her face, breaking them and shattering the memory as she tossed the pieces at the angel monument.

"There's a fine for littering around here."

Frannie looked up to find Patrick Houston

staring down at her. She sighed. If she'd thought he'd follow her, she would have avoided Town Square. Really must remember she lived in a small town now.

He glanced at the empty space on the park bench and said, "May I?"

Wanting to look anywhere but at him, she stared up at the statue of the warrior angel. "It's not advisable."

"I'll take my chances," he said and sat.

"You were warned."

"I must say, it's not every day a beautiful woman storms out of my office. I admit it was rude of me to be late to our appointment. I should have apologized."

"But you didn't, and still aren't." And he had so much to apologize for, yet he continued to act like he didn't know her. Like he didn't remember. Maybe he didn't. God, she was so naïve when it came to men. He probably had picked up so many women in bars that he couldn't keep them all straight. Still, confusion had not been a problem the morning after in the diner. He'd looked guilty as sin and like he had the devil of a hangover.

"Help me out here."

"Let's drop the games, shall we? If you think I'm going to be humiliated in the retelling of what happened, I'm afraid I'll have to disappoint you."

He leaned forward, resting his arms on his knees, palms up. "I'm at a complete loss. Have we met before?"

She turned away and laughed. What an ass.

"Ms. Thompson . . . Frannie, I apologize. It's not my intent to upset or humiliate you in any way. I respected and admired your sister a great deal. I do understand how difficult it is to lose someone close to you."

Frannie wondered how long it would take before people stopped bringing up "her loss" in that sympathetic manner that made her want to scream. No one knew how she felt. No one.

She leaned in as she spoke. "You'll have to excuse me if I'm having a bit of trouble here reconciling your two personas, the upstanding mayor and the drunk. The drunk disgraced himself that night in the bar and took me unwittingly along for the ride." She spoke softly, "Clearly, I was just one of many."

He frowned. "Bar?" He tilted his head, his gaze sweeping her face, her hair, his pale eyes bore into hers. "I'm sorry to say that I used to drink heavily. There are periods, gaps of time, I don't remember." He turned away, but not before she saw the familiar pain flooding his expressive eyes.

He didn't speak for several moments. Didn't look at her. "I'm wracking my brain here. I used to go to a place outside of town to drink. Did I run into you there? I must have," he said to himself without waiting for her to respond.

Frannie crossed her arms and drummed her fingers against her forearm. She should leave. Just get up and walk away, but for reasons she refused to analyze at the moment, she didn't.

"Oh, God," he murmured. "Did I . . . I didn't —" He raked a hand through his hair, and the memory of her hands doing the same rocked her. It was lightly streaked with gray now. Maybe it had been there before, but she hadn't noticed it in the dimly lit bar.

He sighed, looked around, then leaned toward her. The scent of his cologne brought back more memories. It had clung to her skin that night, after.

"Jesus, did I — did we . . ."

She felt her face flush and placed a hand against her neck.

He glanced back at her, then away again. "Oh . . . the night of the blizzard. You were the woman at Jimmy's."

"Yes," she confirmed. So he remembered

32

after all. Well, at least he'd admitted it.

"I thought I'd never see you again."

"But you did, the next day at the diner, and then there was my sister's funeral. So, technically, you've seen me twice."

"Right," he agreed. "But Jenny's been gone six years now. You see, I remember because that's about the same time I found out my wife was seriously ill. I'm afraid I didn't handle getting the prognosis well."

"The relative point is that you were married, something you didn't bother to share with me, and I couldn't have known since I'm not from Angel Ridge." No way was she letting him off the hook for what he'd done. The fact that he was drunk because his wife was sick did not excuse his behavior. "Look, this is not the place to be discussing this. Anyone could walk by and overhear or see us. What if someone tells your wife?" she whispered. "What if *she* sees us?"

She gathered her purse and briefcase and would have stood, but his hand on her arm stopped her.

"Frannie, my wife —" He cleared his throat. "She's gone."

Frannie couldn't breathe, couldn't move. Then, she said, automatically, "I'm sorry."

He turned to face her. "So am I." Then he surprised her by squeezing her hand. That look. That tortured look, mingled with a longing for all he'd lost and regret for mistakes that couldn't be undone, inexplicably made her heart constrict.

Another moment of silent communication passed between them before he stood and walked away.

CHAPTER 2

Patrick walked out of the bright sunshine into the interior of the church, darkened by the hundred-or-more-year-old stained glass windows. He made it a few rows up the aisle before his knees gave way, and he sat heavily in one of the long oak pews. No padded seating for the First Presbyterian Church of Angel Ridge. Padding would hide the polished sheen of the aged oak and provide comfort, which was not a priority. In the town's oldest church, it was more about period look, authenticity. Susan had tried to make things comfortable for Patrick, but all that had changed the day he'd learned his wife would die of cancer before she reached forty.

"Patrick? Is that you back there?"

Reverend Reynolds, the church's pastor, had entered the sanctuary from a side door beside the raised altar where the old, heavy wooden pulpit stood sentinel. When Patrick didn't respond, he walked down the aisle toward him.

"It is you." A few steps closer and he added, "What's happened? How can I help?"

Patrick pulled a hand down his face. He felt numb. Unable to process what had just happened, which he supposed was a blessing. How could he have — he couldn't even form the words in his mind, much less speak them.

Of course he remembered what he'd done that night. Part of it, anyway. There'd been a blizzard, a rarity in East Tennessee. Such a thing was a memorable event. He'd gone out to the edge of town, as he did most nights, to get drunk and kill the pain. It was true; he didn't remember everything that had happened. He'd been too far gone. But he'd remembered enough to recognize Frannie the next day at the diner. The day when his son had wandered off alone and gotten his foot stuck in a storm drain at the hardware store. Patrick had gone to the diner, hung over, desperate for coffee when he saw Frannie, a stranger, just realizing she'd made out with a drunk, *married* man the night before.

He looked up, only just noticing that the preacher had sat on the pew in front of him.

Silent, he waited for Patrick to speak, or not. He was that kind of man. Patient. Understanding that sometimes, silent prayers were more effective than words.

"I wish God had taken me instead of Susan."

"Why would you say that?" Reverend Reynolds said quietly.

Patrick looked up at the wooden beams high above them. "Because she was the better person."

"None of us deserve the blessings God chooses to bestow on us, Patrick."

"Some less than others."

"What's brought this on?"

Patrick sighed. "Another reminder of what an ass I was when I found out Susan was sick. Excuse my language," he added when he realized what he'd said.

"No need to apologize, but we've talked about this, Patrick. No one can fault you for struggling when faced with such grave news about your wife."

"It was quite a bit more than a brief lapse," he mumbled, crossing his arms.

"Patrick, no one knows as well as I do that you became the model of a supportive, kind, loving husband to Susan soon after she became ill. You stood by her, cared for her, loved her to the end. If not for you, I don't know that she would have made it as long as she did after they found the cancer. All the doctors agreed it was a miracle."

"None of the credit's mine, Preacher. She was so determined to beat it."

"For you and your children."

"For the children, yes, but not for me," he said.

Reverend Reynolds linked his fingers and rested his forearms on the back of the pew. "It's been some time since Susan passed. You've struggled, but done well considering all that you've had to take on with caring for the children alone. Are you still attending the grief support group meetings in Knoxville?"

Patrick nodded. Each week, he thought this would be the Thursday he wouldn't go. But when the day came, he found himself driving to the church in the next town and sitting in the same chair. He didn't often talk about his grief, but hearing others share their own made him feel a little less alone in his. A little less like he needed a drink to survive it. Still, he'd leave the grief support group then go straight to an AA meeting, just to be sure. But the pastor didn't know about that. No one did.

"Has something happened, then, to bring back the memory of that time when you felt you'd let your family down?"

Patrick laughed. "I don't think a day goes by that I don't feel that I've let them down."

"Why, Patrick? Why do you feel that when no one else does?"

"Because . . . others were involved."

"Others?"

He closed his eyes. Maybe it was time to talk about it. He needed to talk to someone. Looking up at the kind, older man sitting patiently before him, the words, once started, poured out of him. He told him about the drinking, the anger, the pain, and cheating on his wife. He and Frannie hadn't had sex, but he'd cheated all the same by turning to someone else. He loathed himself even more now for what he'd nearly done. All because he hadn't been strong enough to deal with what was happening to his wife, his family, him.

He slouched down in the pew. "I was such a selfish bastard, thinking only about myself, *my* pain."

"These are normal emotions and re-actions," the pastor said.

"There's no excuse for what I did."

"Did Susan know about your drinking . . . and the rest?"

Patrick nodded, tears clogging his throat and stinging his eyes. "She went with me to

39

my first AA meeting."

"She forgave you, then."

"She did. I didn't deserve her."

"At some point, you must forgive yourself."

"I can't," Patrick said.

"If you want to move forward, out of the
grief and into living the rest of your life,
you must."

He shook his head. "Someone's here. In
Angel Ridge."

"Who?"

"Someone from that time when I was a
drunk. A woman."

"Oh . . ."

"And she's angry. Furious with me for
coming on to her." He looked up then. "She
didn't know I was married. Didn't know
me or Susan. She was a stranger in town
dealing with her own loss, and I made it
worse."

"I don't understand."

"I have to make it right," he continued as
if the preacher hadn't spoken. It was part of
AA's Twelve-Step Program to make amends
with the people he'd harmed. "How do I do
that?"

"First, I think you need to explain what
you just said about her loss and making it
worse."

"She'd just lost her sister when she had the misfortune of running into me at the bar where I chose to numb my pain night after night."

"Oh. Oh, I see. Oh my . . ."

"Right. Jenny Thompson's sister is back in Angel Ridge, and it looks like she's here to stay."

"This is indeed an unforeseen turn of events. Did you ever try to contact her after that time? To make amends?"

"You know about that part of the program?" Patrick asked.

The pastor nodded.

"I didn't know how to contact her, so I did what the program says. Found another way to help. She doesn't know it, but I've been looking after Jenny's house all these years."

"That's good. And, of course, you apologized."

"Yes, but 'I'm sorry' won't cut it. With her moving here, I'm going to have to find a way to deal with this."

"Mmm . . ."

"There's no excuse, no explanation. How can I possibly make this right?"

"Take some time to reflect and meditate on the matter. A way will present itself."

Patrick shook his head. He'd gone over

her plans before going to find her earlier. "She has this idea for revitalizing downtown that will be controversial. With me being the mayor, I'm afraid she'll see me as an adversary."

"Then make sure you're not. This could be just the opportunity you need. What kind of plan does she have in mind?"

"A non-profit that will educate and train unemployed workers, giving them temporary housing and help finding jobs."

"That sounds wonderful," Reverend Reynolds said.

Patrick looked at the pastor. "Have you met the people on the Town Council who will have to approve this?"

"I have, and I see this as the perfect opportunity for you to be a person who can act as a buffer and steer the process to an amenable resolution."

"Nice plan, but I suspect doing that will be just a bit more complicated."

"It always is, son, but you'll find a way. You are a master negotiator. As a politician, dealing effectively with people is your business."

Patrick smiled. "If anything could drive me to drink again, this might do it."

"That's nothing to joke about, Patrick," the reverend said, his tone serious.

The man was right. "Sorry, Pastor."

"Do you have someone to talk to if that desire should overtake you?"

"Yes, I have a sponsor."

"Good. Good," Reynolds said. "If you can't reach that person, I hope you know you can call me."

"I appreciate that."

The pastor stood. "I'll leave you alone then, so you can have some quiet time to consider the situation you find yourself in." He clapped a hand on Patrick's shoulder. "I know you'll do the right thing."

Patrick watched the pastor walk away, wishing he had a fraction of as much confidence in himself.

CHAPTER 3

"Ain't he something?"

Frannie glanced up at the elderly woman who had approached without Frannie noticing. Probably because she was still seething over her encounter with the town's mayor, who had just stood and abruptly left. "Yes. Quite."

The woman sat next to her on the park bench. "I just never get tired of lookin' at him."

The lady sighed, gazing up at the bronze angel before them. Wispy white curls framed her round face, and she wore a long, lightweight blue coat that matched her eyes. Clearly, she had been referring to the angel. He was quite something. A strongly built warrior angel with impressive wings extending from above his shoulders to his feet, he wore a short tunic that revealed muscular legs and arms. His hands clasped a sword's hilt, its tip resting between his sandaled feet.

He looked out across Town Square toward the river below the ridge, keeping vigilant watch over the town that had been named for angels.

"You know, legend has it that an angel saved the town's founders from an Indian attack. That's why they named it Angel Ridge."

"No," Frannie said. "I didn't know. That's interesting."

The older woman nodded. "I'm meeting that nice Craig boy to talk about what kind of flowers I want him to plant here this spring. I always see that flowers are put in around the base of the monument when the seasons change."

Frannie couldn't help smiling. When she looked into the other woman's eyes, Frannie experienced a feeling of peace. Something she definitely needed at the moment.

"Forgive an old woman," she said. "Here I am prattling on about our angel monument and spring flowers when we haven't been properly introduced. I'm Miss Estelee."

Frannie took the woman's extended hand. "Frannie Thompson."

"Oh, you're here at last. It's high time for a pretty young woman like you to come into our town and change some things around a bit. Let me tell you, Angel Ridge is long overdue for looking more outward and less inward. *Mmm-hmm.*"

She leaned back and smiling, returned her attention to the monument.

Puzzled, Frannie said, "I'm due to meet Mr. Craig in a few moments, myself. I had no idea he did landscaping."

"Oh, yes. He's our town handyman."

Frannie frowned. Cole Craig, the renowned architect who specialized in restoration architecture, a handyman? Frannie pointed to a building across the street that housed his offices. "Isn't that Mr. Craig's office?"

The older woman nodded. "That it is."

Frannie just smiled. The poor thing must be a bit confused.

"Your sister stayed with me for a time before she left us," Miss Estelee said.

That comment instantly put Frannie on her guard. A few people in town knew Jenny was alive, but Frannie didn't know who, so she said nothing.

"She was good for Angel Ridge, too," Miss Estelee said, "and now you're here to stir up more trouble and uncover secrets. Yep, I reckon you'll be keepin' us all on our toes." She slapped her leg and laughed. "High time, too. Yep, it's gonna be a spring we'll

46

remember around here for a good long time."

"I beg your pardon?" What was the woman talking about?

"You'll be movin' into your sister's house?"

"Yes. She left it to me."

"And how do your parents feel about losing both their girls?"

Frannie frowned. How did this woman know her parents had no other children? Maybe Jenny had told her. "My father works out of town, and my mother travels quite a bit when he's away. I'm afraid I don't see them much."

"Well, we're sure happy to have you as part of our family here."

"Thank you," Frannie said.

Miss Estelee looked back up at the angel. "I noticed you talking to the Houston boy as I was walking into town just now."

Completely off-balance with the twists and turns in the conversation, Frannie decided to just go along. "Mayor Houston, yes."

The woman turned and speared Frannie with a look that wouldn't let her go. "He's had a hard time, what with his wife being so sick and then her passing. He has a good heart." She tapped her chest with a bent index finger. "Don't judge him too harshly. Folks around here are private when it comes to their personal business, so things ain't always what they seem. You'd do well to remember that when you deal with him and the town folk." She reached out and patted Frannie's hand. "But you're a smart, kind woman with your own secrets, so you know what I'm talking about."

"I'm afraid I'm not following, ma'am," Frannie said, still confused.

"That's all right, honey. You'll find your footing soon enough."

Frannie noticed Cole Craig, Blake Ferguson and Bud DeFoe coming up the sidewalk toward them. She glanced at her watch. Time for her next appointment. She gathered her purse and briefcase, then stood. "I have to be going. It was a pleasure talking to you, ma'am."

"Call me Miss Estelee. Everybody does. Stop by my house anytime for a glass of cold sweet tea. I live in the two-story house on River Road with the wide front porch and the gingerbread trim with angels' wings."

"Thank you."

"Yesiree, you're gonna make your mark on this town, no doubt."

Frannie heard Miss Estelee laughing as she walked across Town Square toward the empty storefronts near the angel monument. This side of the street only had two occupants: Cole Craig's offices and Heart's Desire. The rest of the buildings currently stood empty. If she had anything to say about it, they would soon be occupied.

"Well, here she is now," Mr. DeFoe said. "Angel Ridge's newest entrepreneur."

"Good morning, gentlemen." Frannie shook each man's hand in turn. "Thank you for meeting me."

"It's our pleasure," Mr. DeFoe said. He pulled out a large set of keys and inserted one in the door to the building nearest them. "Let's talk inside."

The men stood to the side as Frannie entered the empty building. This was the building she planned to convert into her office and retail space. The wide, open room had at one time held a dress and millinery store at the turn of the century. Several businesses had come and gone since, but Frannie thought it would be perfect for a thrift shop. They were all the rage with so many struggling to make ends meet. Upstairs, there was plenty of space for the Foundation's offices as well as the job skills training classes she planned to offer.

Frannie placed her purse and briefcase on a table that sat at the side of the room.

"Cole, thank you for getting those revised plans to me so quickly. They were perfect. Exactly what I had in mind."

"Glad to hear it," Cole said.

Now that Frannie thought about it, dressed as he was in jeans and a T-shirt, he could pass as a handyman.

Blake Ferguson handed her a manila envelope. "These are the final figures on construction costs in the three stages we discussed."

"Thank you." The two men were a striking pair. Cole stood around six feet tall and was muscular with long blond hair pulled back into a ponytail, while Blake was a bit taller and lanky with short dark hair. Frannie had met both their wives on previous visits to Angel Ridge, having had business dinners with them to discuss the construction plans. Cole had married Josie Allen, the town librarian, while Blake was married to the town's young new doctor, Janice, whom Frannie would be seeing later in the day. The two men were indeed handsome, but not what she'd call "her type." According to her sister, eligible men in Angel Ridge were scarce and seemed interested in long term relationships. Not what she wanted, even if she did have the time, which she didn't. No, her focus was firmly on this project and remaking her life into something with purpose.

"Did you meet with Patrick?" Cole asked.

"Yes. This morning. I hope you don't mind, but I told him to call you if he had questions about the building plans."

"No problem," Cole said.

"Glad you finally tracked him down," Blake said. "All we need now is approval by the Town Council for those few minor details involving the town ordinances, and we can move forward with obtaining the rest of the building permits."

"The Council's next meeting is less than a week away," Mr. DeFoe said, rubbing his hands together. "Bet there'll be some lively discussions in town this week."

Blake and Cole chuckled.

Frannie looked from one man to the other. "I don't understand."

"Don't get me wrong, Frannie," Bud said. "I'm not saying that what you want to do isn't a wonderful thing for revitalizing the downtown area, but you should understand that this is a small town. People can be set in their ways."

"Some will welcome the change," Blake said. "Others won't."

Frannie smiled. "As much as I'd like unanimous support, I'll be happy with a majority vote in my favor. I have a list of the council members and plan to call on them all this week. Going into the meeting, I'd like to know what to expect."

"You'll have no trouble getting the support of Doc Prescott and Dixie. It's Harriet McKay and Jim Wallace you'll need to win over," Mr. DeFoe warned. "You should also know that in the case of a tie, the mayor is the deciding vote."

That gave her a moment's pause, but she said, "Not to worry. My father was a career politician. I learned from a master how to win people to one's way of thinking."

"No disrespect to your father," Cole said, "but it's likely he never came up against Harriet McKay. She's guided matters in this town for most of her adult life. When she sets her mind against something, she can dig in her heels."

"And sometimes she digs in her heels just to stir up trouble," Bud grumbled.

"But she can be gotten around," Blake added. "You proved that, Cole."

"Money won that battle. My firm's donation to the library's foundation got that computer wing built."

"Good, then we should have no problem," Frannie said. "This plan is fully funded and will bring a significant cash influx to the town's economy, not to mention the good press that this philanthropic endeavor will generate."

"That's another matter. The town newspaper hasn't been the same since we lost your sister, God rest her soul," Bud said.

"Who's running it now?" Frannie asked.

"The church ladies," Blake and Cole said in unison.

"The church ladies?"

"Mrs. McKay and her cronies, Thelma Houston and Geraldine Wallace. They mean well —" Blake began.

"No, they don't," Mr. DeFoe interrupted. "They *mean* to do exactly what Mrs. McKay tells them, and they don't even have a passing acquaintance with the concept of impartial reporting."

"Wallace and Houston?" Frannie said. "Any relation to the sheriff and the mayor?"

"They're sisters," Bud said. "One is Grady's mother, the other is Patrick's." Bud held up his hands and added, "Please don't misunderstand what we're saying here. They're nice ladies away from Harriet."

Blake and Cole both nodded their agreement. Frannie really needed to move on hiring an administrative assistant. It would be advantageous to find someone from town who could give her all the insider information she needed on how to navigate the social and political landscape.

"Another thing about your plan," Bud pointed out, "is it'll bring a lot of outsiders into a town that doesn't always take to strangers."

Frannie's smile stayed in place. "All of the people who come into town as part of the job rehabilitation program will have had a thorough background check by the sheriff, and they will be temporary residents."

"Unless they decide to stay," Cole said.

Blake looked up at the ceiling and rocked back on his heels, hands in his pockets. "I can hear Mrs. McKay now as she expounds on the dangers of transients and the dregs of society in our midst."

"God save us," Cole said with a big smile, holding a hand over his heart.

Frannie put the manila envelope Blake had given her into her briefcase. "I've yet to meet a society maven I can't win over."

"I like your confidence, little lady," Mr. DeFoe said. "Reminds me of your sister. She had spunk. We sure do miss her."

Everyone turned as someone walked into the building. Frannie tensed as Patrick Houston joined them.

"Pardon the interruption," he said as he nodded to the men, his gaze finally resting on Frannie's. "Ms. Thompson, I had a quick look at your plans. Very ambitious."

"An excellent opportunity for Angel Ridge," she countered. "A venture that will benefit everyone involved."

"Yes, perhaps." He hesitated. "But something of this nature will require a bit of consideration and discussion for the Town Council as well as the town's residents."

"I'm happy to go over my plans with anyone who has an interest in the project."

"Good. I'm recommending that the next meeting of the Town Council be pushed back a few weeks."

"A few weeks?" Frannie said.

"A project of this magnitude can be most beneficial to the town if it has the full support of the community and its businesses. You've clearly been planning this for some time, but the town is just hearing about it. I understand your desire to begin right away, and I support that, but it will take a month or more —"

"A month!" Frannie exclaimed.

"Maybe less, if there's no serious opposition," Patrick finished. "I'd recommend a Town Hall style meeting to encourage support and allow residents and business owners to ask questions and raise any concerns."

Frannie took a deep breath and counted

while she waited for her heart rate to slow. Unfortunately, she needed the mayor's support for this to all go smoothly. Her personal issues with him aside, this was business. She could not afford to alienate him. "That's a wonderful idea. I'll contact your assistant to schedule something as soon as possible."

"Excellent. Karen is copying your plans so they can be couriered to the council members right away."

Frannie gritted her teeth, but managed to smile. "Thank you." She didn't need the backing of the community to go forward with her plan, but she also did not want their opposition. Fortunately, she had planned to implement her program in stages, beginning with opening the thrift shop and her administrative offices. Next, she could run the job training classes upstairs while the other buildings were being renovated.

"This is good. It'll give us time to close on the sale of the property before the meetings."

"Do you think that's wise?" Patrick asked.

"I don't know what you mean," Frannie said evenly.

"If the Town Council does not approve your requests, it could mean trouble. You'd be stuck with all this real estate and nothing to do with it."

"Thank you for your concern, but if the Town Council does not approve our requests, I feel confident that we'll be able to make any needed modifications to the plans so we can move forward." Frannie turned to the other men in the room. "Gentlemen, thank you for coming. I know you're busy. I don't want to keep you."

"Do you still want to meet tomorrow morning about scheduling when the renovations will begin?" Blake asked.

"Yes."

Frannie did not miss Patrick's frown, but she chose to ignore it.

"Let me know if there's anything you need," Cole said as he offered her his hand.

"That goes for me, too," Mr. DeFoe said. He gave her the keys to the buildings. "Here, might as well take these."

"Are you sure?" Frannie said.

"Absolutely. The property's as good as yours."

"Thank you," Frannie said, dropping the keys into her briefcase. The men filtered out of the building, all except for Patrick Houston.

"Was there something further, Mayor?"

"Yes. First, I want to apologize for what happened between us, *um,* before. I don't expect you to forgive me right away, but I hope you'll give me the opportunity to prove that my apology is sincere."

Frannie crossed her arms and stared at the toes of her shoes showing beneath her slacks before raising her gaze to his. "The only thing I need from you is your co-operation and support as it pertains to my business venture in Angel Ridge."

A look of regret flickered across his eyes and settled in the lines of his face, lines a man so young shouldn't have. "I under-stand. To that end, I'd like to go over the proposed business plan with you so that I can have a more thorough understanding of it."

"Of course," Frannie agreed.

"Since you seem to want to start up right away, I'd like to meet soon."

"Unfortunately, my day is full. I'll call your assistant to set something up."

"Would you be willing to discuss this over dinner at Ferguson's tonight?"

"Dinner?" she said without thinking, hop-ing that word hadn't sounded as panicked as she felt. She most definitely did not want to go anywhere with this man that was outside an environment she could not con-trol.

"You have to eat," he said.

His smile was easy and charming. Her breath hitched in her chest, and she had to swallow hard against the distracting feelings he evoked as well as the memories of those lips on hers. Good Lord . . . She needed time to come to grips with this situation, but she also needed to get him on board with her plan. This was too important. She'd worked too hard to back down now at the first sign of adversity. She could do this. They'd only shared a kiss. They should both act like adults and move on.

"All right. Dinner at Ferguson's to discuss my business plan," she said firmly. "Will six work for you?"

"Yes." His smile widened, flooding his eyes with life. "See you then."

He turned and walked out of the building. Frannie pressed a hand to her chest and let out her breath in a whoosh. She had to meet with Patrick to go over her plans. This was strictly business. She looked at her watch to gauge how much time she had before that dinner. What had happened between them had been a mistake, but her body still reacted to him. Strongly.

If she strengthened her resolve and repeated over and over for the rest of the day that this is business and nothing more, maybe by the time six o'clock came, she'd walk into the diner and feel nothing but an overwhelming desire to convince the mayor to support her foundation.

"I'm so sorry I'm late. I'm Frannie Thompson. I had an appointment at 4:30," she said in a rush to the nurse sitting behind the reception desk. The doctor's office in Angel Ridge was actually a house on Ridge Road. The downstairs held a reception area and examination rooms. Frannie wondered if the doctor lived upstairs.

The woman wearing a traditional white nurse's dress said, "The doctor has a busy schedule."

"I completely understand," Frannie said. "I'm happy to leave my medical records and reschedule."

"Did I hear the door, Mable?"

Janice Thornton Ferguson walked into the room. The strikingly beautiful woman, tall with long blond hair, came forward smiling. "Oh, good. I'm so glad I didn't miss you." She extended a hand. "It's good to see you again, Frannie."

Frannie took her hand, shaking it. "Thank you, Dr. Ferguson. I'm sorry I'm late."

"Call me Janice, please. And no worries. You're my last appointment today. Come on back."

60

The nurse gave Frannie a look with raised brows that said timeliness was next to Godliness as far as *she* was concerned. "Would you like me to take the patient's vitals, Doctor?"

"Thank you, Mable," Janice said, "but I think we'll be fine. Why don't you go home early?"

"Who would answer the phones until five?" the nurse asked.

"Forward them to the service. They'll page me if there's an emergency."

"Yes, Doctor." Reluctantly, the nurse stood, gathering her things to leave.

"Let's go to my office, shall we?" Janice said, motioning toward an open door to her left. It was a large office with tall, wood plank ceilings and floor to ceiling bookcases lining the walls. Tall, multi-paned windows let in the bright sunlight. A large mahogany desk stood in the center of the room. The doctor had diplomas indicating that she'd graduated with honors from Radford and then received her medical degree from Johns Hopkins, also with honors. "Won't you have a seat?"

"Thank you," Frannie said. "I have to say, you're not at all who I would expect to find working as a doctor in such a small town."

Sitting behind the desk in a tufted leather

chair, Janice said, "Believe me, no one was as surprised as I was. I had a successful practice in Knoxville before my uncle, Dr. Charles Prescott, convinced me to take over his practice so he could retire."

"I believe Jenny mentioned him." How could Frannie forget? Jenny had told her the town doctor was an older man who looked like Santa.

"After coming here, I couldn't resist the charm of the town." She held up a hand showing Frannie a wedding band and engagement ring. "It didn't hurt that I fell in love and got married here as well. I can't believe we'll celebrate our fifth anniversary this year."

"Congratulations," Frannie smiled. "I'm going to enjoy working with Blake on the renovations."

"He's told me about your plans for the non-profit. I'd like to become involved. Perhaps we could discuss that at another time over a cup of coffee?"

"I'd like that," Frannie smiled, settling into the doctor's easy manner.

"Good." Janice leaned back in her chair, linking her hands in front of her. "So, this is just a visit to establish you as a new patient?"

"Yes. I have my medical records." Frannie

removed a thick, heavy folder from her briefcase and handed it across the desk to the doctor.

"Wow." Looking down at the folder then back at Frannie, Janice said, "This might take a while to get through. Why don't you give me the short version?"

Frannie nodded, swallowing. Even after all this time, it was difficult saying the words out loud. "When I was a teenager, I had acute lymphocytic leukemia."

CHAPTER 4

Frannie waited for the sympathy to flood the young doctor's green eyes, but not shocked at all, Janice said, "I see. You look quite healthy. I assume you achieved remission?"

"Yes. Permanent remission."

"Excellent. Any long-term side effects from the cancer or the treatments? I assume you had initial treatment, achieved remission, and then had subsequent treatments in cycles over the next several years?"

"Yes. I had a bone marrow transplant —"

"From a family member or a non-related donor?"

"Family member, my sister. I went into remission within a year of diagnosis, which was optimal." The doctor nodded as she took notes. "Then I had three more courses of treatment over the next two years to prevent recurrence."

"Anything else I should know?"

"No, nothing that needs discussing now. It's all in the records."

The doctor sat back smiling. "I can see you take very good care of yourself. Any current complaints?"

"Lately, I've noticed that my endurance is a little off. I jog for exercise, but for the past few weeks, I get fatigued sooner than normal."

Dr. Ferguson stood and came around the desk. "There could be a lot of reasons for that — many of which can be easily fixed. You've just moved, and you've been working long hours getting settled in your home and setting up your business. But let's do an examination and draw some blood. It could be something as simple as an iron deficiency." As they walked out of the office to an examination room, the doctor asked, "Has this ever happened before?"

"Not that I can recall, not for this length of time anyway."

"All right." She opened a drawer in the base of the examination table. "Change into this gown, and we'll have a look."

"Doctor?"

"Janice," she corrected.

Frannie smiled, liking the woman's easy, laid back manner, but that worried her a bit. "Janice, this is a small town, and I'm new here. I have no doubt that you will keep this confidential, but I really don't want anyone to know about this." She paused, gathering her thoughts while Janice waited patiently. "You see, I come from a place where everyone around me knew I'd had cancer, and as a result, I was treated differently — carefully. One of the reasons I moved was because I wanted a fresh start. I hope things can be different here."

"I understand." Janice put a hand on her shoulder. "I'll do whatever I can do to see that you live a full life here in Angel Ridge, unencumbered by this past illness. When you come for office visits, if you'd like, use the back entrance, and my nurse will take you directly to an examination room. I'd also be happy to see you after hours, so you won't run into other patients."

Relieved that she understood, Frannie felt her shoulders lower with the lifting of that concern. "Thank you."

"Think nothing of it. One of the benefits of practicing medicine in such a small town is that I can focus on the needs of my patients. I find that I really enjoy that aspect of my job."

Frannie nodded, but still, she had to ask. "What about your nurse?"

Janice laughed, sliding her hands into the

pockets of her short, white clinical jacket. "No worries there. Mable is a veritable Fort Knox. I've done my best to get her to loosen up a bit, but she's a taskmaster, constantly on me about following proper protocol. As you may have noticed, she refers to me only as 'Doctor.' I can't get her to call me anything else."

Frannie's smile widened. "I think this is going to work out just fine."

When Frannie walked into the diner later that evening, her heart was pounding so hard, she felt lightheaded. She could attribute the reaction to nerves, but she didn't get nervous in a business meeting. Frannie always felt confident when it came to what she did. Only in her personal life did she feel inadequate. Growing up sick, she didn't have the experience with men most women her age could boast. Patrick Houston was just another reminder of that.

The man in question stood and approached. He was dressed casually in jeans and a dark blue polo shirt that made his hair look darker. In stark contrast, his pale eyes drew her in. He held out his hand. She took it in what should have been a professional exchange, but given what had transpired between them and the attraction still

67

shimmering just below the surface, it was anything but. When their hands touched, an electric charge shot up her arm making her shiver in reaction.

"Ms. Thompson. Thank you for meeting me," he said.

"My pleasure," she said automatically, but the word "pleasure" sent her mind in a whole different direction. Her voice sounded like someone else's — breathy and less than business-like.

He extended an arm toward the booth where he'd been sitting and ushered her in that direction with a hand hovering at the small of her back. Even though he didn't touch her, she felt his nearness like a caress. She slid into the booth and looked around the quaint diner. Light green linoleum tabletops with daisies in vases and darker green vinyl booths lined walls of the long, narrow dining area. A lunch counter near the entrance had stools where overflow customers sat. Every booth was taken.

Frannie forced a smile. "Popular spot."

"Always," Patrick agreed. "There are only a couple of restaurants around here, so there's not a lot of choice in where to eat out, unless you drive to Maryville or Knoxville. But don't worry, the food here is excellent."

He acted as if she'd never been in Ferguson's Diner. Probably just as well. Hopefully, they'd said everything that needed saying about "the incident."

Frannie opened the menu just as Dixie Ferguson approached and stood next to their table, a hand cocked on her hip. Frannie looked up. The woman was striking — tall, thin but shapely, she wore a crisp white blouse and a short dark skirt. Tall, red sandals with wedge heels matched a red apron and the layered red beads at her neck. Her most striking feature was short spiked hair a vibrant shade of red that put Frannie in mind of flames shooting from her head. That was her first warning.

"Well, well. We are truly fortunate this evening. The mayor of our fair town graces us with his presence."

"Dixie," Patrick said. "Good to see you."

"Mmm-hmm." Her gaze swung to Frannie. "Frannie Thompson. I wasn't aware you were in town. Welcome back."

She said the words, but Frannie got the distinct impression they were just that. Words.

"Hello, Dixie. So nice to see you again."

"What brings you to town?"

All right. Skipping the pleasantries, let's just get down to it. "Actually, I've moved into

69

my sister's house. I'm relocating to Angel Ridge."

Dixie looked from Frannie to Patrick and back to Frannie. "Really," she said flatly. "Well, isn't that nice."

She emphasized the last word in a way that let Frannie know she didn't actually think it was nice. What was with her? What could Frannie have possibly done to upset Dixie Ferguson? The last time they'd spoken, Frannie had felt that she and the woman were on good terms. That there might actually be a possibility of them becoming friends. But that had been years before, so she had no idea what could have happened to change that. Dixie Ferguson was not a person to have as an enemy. She knew everyone in town, was well liked and respected as a businesswoman, and she was a member of the Town Council.

Patrick spoke up. "Ms. Thompson plans to open a non-profit in town. The plans should have been couriered over to you today."

Dixie waved her hand. "Yes. Karen dropped something off around the time the lunch crowd hit, but I haven't had a chance to look them over."

Fully capable of speaking for herself, Frannie said, "I'd appreciate the opportunity to sit down with you to go over what I have planned. I'm looking to partner with businesses in town for job training."

Dixie shifted her weight and focused her gaze somewhere over Frannie's head. "I'll check my schedule."

An older, dark-haired woman, who was a little on the plump side, walked up and stood next to Dixie smiling at Patrick and then Frannie. "Hello, Patrick."

Patrick rose, put his arm around the woman and kissed her cheek. "Mom. I didn't know you were here, or I would have said 'hello.' "

His mother leaned into Patrick's side, patting his shoulder. "Well, that's all right, honey. I'm just here having a bite to eat with your Aunt Geraldine."

Patrick looked around and, finding his aunt, held up a hand in greeting.

"Who's your young lady?" his mother asked.

Frannie nearly groaned. The last thing she wanted was people pairing her with Patrick.

Patrick swung his gaze to hers and rushed to explain. "Mom, this is Frannie Thompson. We're having a *business* dinner to discuss her plans for a new business in town." Patrick put the emphasis on "business" and said the word twice, but that

71

seemed to have no effect on his mother. "Frannie, this is my mother, Thelma Houston."

"Thompson? Any relation to Jenny?" the woman asked.

"Yes, she was my sister," Frannie said.

"Oh, you poor dear." She walked around Dixie and slid into the booth next to Frannie. Surprised, Frannie scooted over to make room. "I'm so, so sorry. The town loved your sister. We do miss her."

Frannie looked up at Patrick, who just shrugged and sat back down. She thought she heard Dixie mumble, "If it ain't one thing, it's your mother," and then in a stronger voice, "What can I get y'all to drink?"

"Water's fine," Frannie said.

"I'll have sweet tea," Patrick said.

Dixie nodded. "The special is butter beans and cornbread. Abby will be your server." She smiled, or more accurately, curled her lips. "Y'all have a nice night."

Frannie watched Dixie walk away, looked back at Patrick and then at his mother, who was speaking.

"You know, my sister and I have taken over running the paper," Mrs. Houston said.

"Is that right?" Frannie didn't see any reason to tell Mrs. Houston that someone had mentioned it to her already.

"Yes, well, it's not near the publication your sister did. It's more like a town newsletter that highlights current events, upcoming meetings, obituaries, marriages and births."

"I'm sure Jenny would be glad you and your sister took that on."

"Well, we're happy to do it, dear," she said, patting Frannie's leg. She seemed like a genuinely nice person that Frannie could have liked, if she weren't Patrick's mother. That fact made this extremely awkward.

"We could run an article about your new business," Mrs. Houston offered. "Perhaps you'd have time for an interview?"

"Of course. That would be wonderful," Frannie said. Reaching into her purse, she handed the woman a business card. "Just give me a call, and we'll set something up."

"Thank you, Frannie. Well, I won't stay since the two of you have, what was it you said, dear? *Business* to discuss?" The dark-haired woman raised her eyebrows when she said the word, her eyes twinkling.

Frannie nearly groaned.

Patrick sighed and stood, offering his mother a hand as she slid out of the booth. He leaned down and kissed her again.

"Lovely to meet you, Frannie," Mrs.

Houston said.

"Nice to meet you, as well, ma'am."

To Patrick, the woman said, "I'll talk to you soon."

"I look forward to it." As his mother walked away, Patrick sat again. "Sorry about that."

"No apology necessary. She's a lovely woman."

"She's a nosy woman," he corrected, "but thank you for not pointing it out."

"She's a mother. Goes with the territory."

Patrick couldn't help how his gaze lingered on Frannie. She looked good. Too good. She'd changed out of the business suit she'd worn earlier, exchanging it for a green, cotton dress with a thin white sweater. The neckline was high, scooping just below her neck. She wore a simple strand of pearls, and her long, thick reddish brown hair was pulled back into a ponytail, revealing matching pearl studs in her earlobes. The look was demure, but her lush body launched his imagination into overdrive.

He wished he could remember more about the kiss they'd shared. Maybe then he wouldn't be so curious about sampling her shiny pink lip gloss. He wondered if it tasted like cherries or strawberries . . . What was it they said? Forbidden fruit was always the sweetest. Something in the back of his mind reminded him that it was no longer forbidden. He was free now. But past transgressions stood in the way.

Frannie had picked up the menu and studied it intently, oblivious to the direction of his thoughts.

"What do you recommend?" she asked.

"Pick anything. There isn't a bad choice on the menu."

Abby approached the table and set a glass of iced water in front of Frannie. His daughter had dyed her strawberry blond hair black, against his wishes, but the light roots were showing. He'd like to say she looked like her mother, but she'd never looked much like him or Susan.

"Are you ready to order?" she asked Frannie.

Frannie gave Abby a sweet, gentle smile that touched her dark blue eyes. He wished she could look at him that way.

"I'll have the grilled chicken salad with house vinaigrette on the side."

She nodded and scribbled on her order pad. "What are you having, Dad?"

Frannie looked at him, surprised. "Abby, this is Frannie Thompson. Frannie, this is my daughter, Abby."

She turned and smiled at his daughter

again. "I'm pleased to meet you, Abby."

Abby didn't respond. To cover the awkward silence, Patrick said, "Frannie is Jenny Thompson's sister. She's just moved to Angel Ridge."

Abby just nodded. "So, are you eating or not? I have other tables to check on."

"I'll have meatloaf with mashed potatoes, green beans and rolls."

More scribbling, then she took their menus and walked toward the kitchen to turn in their orders.

"Sorry," Patrick said. "I wish I could say she's usually more pleasant."

Frannie shrugged. "She's a teenager."

Patrick nodded, embarrassed that Frannie had witnessed the awkward exchange between him and his daughter.

"You must have been awfully young when she was born," Frannie commented as she sipped her water.

"Right out of high school," he confirmed.

"She's lovely."

"Thank you. She's had a tough time since Susan passed. They were close."

Frannie nodded and looked everywhere but at him. Bad move bringing up Susan, considering. Good Lord, talking to this woman was like navigating a field of landmines. Better to stick to the business at hand.

"I had a closer look at your plans this afternoon. Quite an ambitious undertaking."

"It is, but I think planning and the right staff, as well as the support of the town — particularly its businesses — will make the process seamless."

She had a way of spinning the negative to a positive. "I'd like to hear more about the timing in the implementation of the project phases."

Frannie folded her hands on the table and smiled that fake smile that was meant to put him at ease, but didn't have the desired effect. Some devil inside him wanted to rattle her, wanted to see her flustered and passionate like she'd been this morning. He wished he had a clearer memory of the woman who had returned his advances in a bar. Just the thought of kissing her . . .

"The first phase of the project will begin immediately, in the building where we stood earlier today. The downstairs area will be a thrift shop, with the Foundation's administrative offices and space for job training upstairs."

"Will that work begin before the Town Council has the opportunity to endorse the entire plan?"

Same smile in place, she said, "The retail space won't open immediately, but administrative space, as well as a presence in town, is critical at this juncture."

"And if the Town Council doesn't back your plan?"

"Are you saying you don't believe they'll put their full support behind a project that will help put people who are out of work back into the workforce and supporting the local economy?"

"I think the Council, along with some town residents, may have concerns about the people the program will bring to Angel Ridge. This is a small community populated primarily by the descendants of a few families whose ancestors founded the town in the late 1700s. Let's just say, it takes some people time to warm to outsiders and new ideas."

"Yes, I've heard. Be assured that the people who apply to the program will undergo a strenuous application process that will include a background check as well as extensive interviews. We will be looking for people who have held long-term employment, but have fallen victim to the downsizing that has negatively affected the manufacturing and retail sectors of the economy."

"It looks like your focus will be on retail."

"Yes. Two of the buildings I'm filling were once retail businesses in Angel Ridge. I want to see them vibrant once again with more viable retail outlets."

"And a bed and breakfast?"

"Yes. I was quite surprised to learn that there's no hotel in Angel Ridge. The B&B will fill that need and invite tourists to stay here once they come to visit the town."

"That's where the interpretation of the ordinance regarding housing in the business district comes into play."

"Yes," Frannie said.

Patrick nodded. "What types of job training will you be doing?"

"Computer skills for people who may want to start their own small business, as well as skilled labor apprenticeships. With so many pursuing college educations, there has become a market shortage of skilled workers. We will be using people in both areas as we set up the Foundation and renovate the buildings. With the B&B, we can also train people to serve in the hospitality industry. Additionally," Frannie added, "I'm hoping to partner with businesses in town who can help us with job training in other areas."

Abby brought their food, refilled their

drinks and left.

"Thanks, hon," Patrick said to his daughter's retreating back. Returning his attention to Frannie, he said, "That's a lot of change, in a short amount of time, for such a small town." He tucked into the meatloaf and mashed potatoes. Having skipped lunch, he was starved.

"It's an opportunity to create positive change for the community."

Patrick wiped his mouth with his napkin. "You're a master at spinning anything in your favor."

"I choose to see obstacles as opportunities."

Patrick lifted his chin, observing her as he chewed. She was chasing salad around her plate with a fork, but hadn't yet taken a bite. The devil inside made him ask, "Does that apply to all areas of your life or just business?"

She set her fork aside, took a deep breath and sipped her water before responding. "I can't see how that's relevant to our discussion, Mayor."

"Patrick. We're very informal in Angel Ridge. Along those lines, can I give you some advice?"

"Of course," she said, but caution laced her words.

"I appreciate that you're educated and have thoroughly thought out your plan, but when you present this at the Town Hall Meeting, you might want to use plainer language. Otherwise, people might read you as too slick."

"Excuse me?"

"When you talk about this, you sound kind of like a lawyer or a salesman. By that I mean, you have an answer for everything, and you put a positive spin on anything that could be construed as negative."

"I don't understand the problem."

"I'm just saying that people here have a basic mistrust of those kinds of people."

"Lawyers and sales people," she said.

"Right."

She raised an eyebrow. "People also have a basic mistrust of politicians."

Patrick smiled. "True enough." He was enjoying their verbal exchange a little too much, which made him want to push a little harder, just to probe around to see if there was a chink in her armor. "How's your salad?"

She looked at the plate in front of her like she'd just noticed it was there. "Oh, I haven't tried it yet."

"Go ahead. I won't ask any more questions for now, if that'll make you feel more comfortable."

Frannie insisted, "I'm not uncomfort-able."

Patrick leaned in, looking to his left and right before quietly confiding, "I wish I could say the same. I can't remember being this uncomfortable in quite some time."

Frannie pressed her back against the seat. "Please don't do that."

"What?"

She looked around this time. "Do anything that would make it appear that we're having an intimate conversation."

Now she was uncomfortable, and again, it was his fault, but he couldn't seem to stop baiting her. "People are going to think what they will."

Placing her napkin on the table, she scooted out of the booth. "Then this was a mistake," she said before turning to walk out of the diner.

"Damn it," he mumbled as he scrambled to catch up to her in front of the building. "Frannie —"

She spun to face him. "Don't follow me," she said, then immediately turned again and increased her pace.

Ignoring her request, he got close enough to grasp her arm, halting her progress. "What was that?" he asked.

"I don't want even the hint of impropriety in our relationship."

"Then don't make a scene by storming out of the only eating establishment in town while we're having a business dinner."

She moved her arm out of his loose grasp and started walking again. "You made it impossible for me to stay."

"You certainly lay a lot of blame at my feet."

She stopped and looked back at him, her face flushed and a hand on her hip. Fire flashed from her dark blue eyes. Lord, she was stunning.

"You created this situation. If you hadn't kissed me that night," she moved her hand back and forth between them, "having a business relationship now wouldn't be a problem."

"And yet you've returned to the scene of the crime, so to speak."

"What's that supposed to mean?"

He took her arm and guided her to the side of the building to get them off the sidewalk and away from curious stares. "I'm not proud of my behavior, and I'm not excusing it. All I can do is apologize for it, which I've done. But let's call a spade a spade, shall we? You were at a bar that night, in the middle of a blizzard, and a willing participant in that kiss when you don't seem like the type. It begs the question, why?"

She folded her arms defensively. "I don't owe you any explanations. Furthermore, I won't appease your conscience by giving you my forgiveness and wiping the slate clean for something that was unforgivable."

Night was falling softly around them. The constable would soon be lighting the old-fashioned, oil burning streetlamps that lined Main Street's brick sidewalks. People were tucked in their houses, living normal lives. How he envied them.

"It was just a kiss," he said softly. Or was it? For her to have such a strong reaction after so many years had passed, it must have rocked her world. That made him want to kiss her again now, even more.

"You were married."

"I guess you didn't notice my wedding band."

That gave her a moment's hesitation before she responded. "I didn't."

Patrick sighed. Blame it on the alcohol. "Have you never done anything that you regretted, Frannie?" he asked. "Something for which you didn't deserve forgiveness, but wished for it anyway? Not to ease the guilt you feel, because trust me, the guilt is a demon that won't leave me alone. The forgiveness is so you know that the person giving it has gotten past what you did."

Frannie focused on the intensity in his eyes, giving what he'd said some thought. She almost wished she could say she had done something that needed forgiving. The sad truth was that because she'd been gravely ill and survived, she'd taken care to stay safe and do what was expected of her. Any time she'd ventured to do anything out of character or something that involved taking risks, she'd regretted it, including the one time she'd kissed a stranger in a bar. That was something she regretted — that and the fact she'd wasted the years since her illness playing it safe. In both instances, the only person she had to blame was herself. She didn't want to be afraid to live her life, but fear had been her constant companion for many, many years.

When she didn't respond, he said, "It must be nice to have lived a life with no regrets."

"I didn't say that I don't have regrets. I regret having been in that bar and kissing you."

"And we've come full circle with the blame lying at my feet."

"Okay. If it makes you happy, I'll accept my part of the responsibility. I was in a bar getting drunk, and that impaired my judgment to the point that I kissed a total stranger, who was drunker than I was." She laughed. "People get drunk and hook up in bars all the time. Leave it to me to find a married man the one time I do it."

"You were drinking that night because you'd lost your sister."

"Yes. I wanted something to ease the pain and help me stop thinking about losing her," she admitted. "And you were drinking because your wife was terminally ill. I suppose the excuses make it all okay if we can understand the 'why' of it."

"You're wrong on two counts. First, nothing makes what I did okay. And second, I was drinking that night because I'm an alcoholic. Even if my wife hadn't been ill, I would have been drunk anyway."

CHAPTER 5

"I wish I could say that my wife becoming terminally ill was enough for me to get clean, but the truth is that the incident with my son wandering off the day after the blizzard spurred me to do it. My wife *always* deserved better than I gave her. She was so strong, so independent. She managed our family without any help from me. When she got sick, for the first time, *she* needed *me.* My kids needed me, but I didn't step up even then."

"Did she forgive you?" Frannie asked. If she had been his wife in the same circumstances, she'd have left him long before becoming ill.

"Yes. That was Susan — so forgiving and understanding of human imperfection. Like I said, I didn't deserve her. None of us did. Maybe that's why God took her so young."

Hearing that statement, Frannie felt herself soften toward him. She had intimate knowledge about living in the shadow of someone she could never quite measure up to. Jenny had always been larger than life and adventurous, doing things that kept Frannie and their mother in a constant state of worry. *"I'm just so glad I don't have to worry about you, dear,"* their mother would say to Frannie. *"I don't know what I'd do if I had two Jennys."*

But secretly, Frannie had always longed to take chances. Being sick had taken choices from her, but after she'd gotten well, she'd had no excuse for going the safe route. She'd chosen interior design as her boring vocation while Jenny had chosen journalism as her means of affecting change in the world. Through investigative reporting, she would dive into any number of dangerous situations, a tireless crusader for the truth. Ultimately, her fearlessness had taken her from her family. She'd uncovered a crime ring that wanted her dead, requiring her to give up the life she'd known and go into the Witness Security Program. All with no regrets.

Frannie still hadn't forgiven her sister for leaving her alone in a life she could no longer tolerate. How could this man expect her to forgive him for a mistake made at a time when she was vulnerable and just beginning to deal with losing her sister? People like Jenny and Patrick lived their lives in whatever way they chose without regard to the damage they caused the people in their lives. And yet, he stood before her saying he had made a change — that he was now a different person, and she didn't know what to do with that.

"You're sober now?" she asked.

He pulled his sobriety coin out of his pocket and showed it to her. "I haven't had a drink since that night we met."

Frannie took in what he'd said, absorbing the meaning behind his words. He realized what a terrible mess he'd made of his life and seemed determined to make a change. She had to admire that, at least a little.

He smiled. "Since I've been sober, I've learned that not drinking isn't the hard part. The hard part is realizing everything you missed while you were drunk, all the time you can't get back, and that making amends isn't about an apology made and forgiveness given. It's about being present and sober every day to prove to the ones you hurt that you're here, really here, and willing to do the work to be in their lives now and in the future."

"But you don't have that chance with your wife."

"No," he said, regret lacing his words. "But I have our children. I can be here for them."

Frannie looked at the ground, wanting to ask a question, but not sure she should. Not sure it mattered, but she needed to know. For herself. "Can I ask you a question?"

"Yes." His response was immediate. Certain.

"That night with me in the bar, was that the only time you —"

"Yes. I'd never cheated on Susan before."

"Why do you think it happened, with me?"

Before answering, Patrick rubbed the dark stubble on his jaw. "Do you really want me to answer that? Do I need to?"

Frannie frowned, confused by his response. "Of course." If she was going to deal with this, she had to understand why it had happened just once, with her.

He took a step forward, invading her space with his warmth, scent and presence. His fingers slid up her arm to her neck, his thumb at her jaw moved back and forth, hitching her pulse into overdrive.

"There's something . . . intense between us," he breathed near her ear.

"No," she said automatically, pressing back against the rough, brick wall behind her.

"With our normal responses dulled by liquor, that kiss was an automatic response we couldn't deny."

He brushed the back of his fingers up and down her neck, triggering a memory of his mouth, hot and moist, pressed there that night so long ago. Now sober, she was even more vulnerable to him and her own re-action because she realized what was hap-pening, and she chose to allow it by not moving away from his touch.

His lips almost touched hers, but stayed a frustrating breath away. He framed her face with his hands, and she eased hers up his chest. Good Lord, she'd never wanted to kiss a man more than she did Patrick at this moment. So much so that nothing else mat-tered. Nothing.

He leaned away from her, then took a couple of steps back. When several feet separated them, reason began to slowly re-turn.

"I wish attraction was enough . . ." he said, shoving his hands into his pockets.

"But it doesn't change anything," she fin-ished.

"Oh, it changes everything. We just haven't figured out how to navigate it."

"Or if we should navigate it. I mean, I don't want you to support my business plan because of it."

"I wouldn't do that. I'll give your plan my support on its own merit. It's a good thing for Angel Ridge and all the people it will help."

Frannie managed a smile. "Thank you."

He nodded. "But don't expect the rest of the Council, or the town for that matter, to give it their support. It's going to be a hard sale."

"You know what they say. Anything worthwhile is worth fighting for."

"It certainly is." He smiled then, a genuine smile that lent a warm light to his pale eyes. She'd been talking about her business, but she wondered if he'd taken what she'd said as a personal challenge.

"Good night, Frannie."

He turned and walked away, leaving her off-balance and facing some hard questions. Had she come to town because of Jenny, to honor her work here with this foundation, or had she come here as Patrick had suggested, because of that one unforgettable encounter with him? In the back of her mind, had she been secretly holding out hope that she'd find him again? Now that he was single, no barrier prevented them from exploring this attraction, but it was messy. She had work to do, a town to win over and a business to get off the ground. That left little room for anything else. And there was the fact that she was a cancer survivor. Patrick would be crazy to get involved with someone that had a history of cancer given what he'd been through.

Frannie rubbed her hands up and down her arms, willing away the lingering sensations from his touch. But her body refused to cooperate. Her mind shouted all the reasons why the two of them together was a bad idea, while being close to him made it impossible not to consider what it might be like to give in.

Frannie arrived home wound up. So she changed out of her dress into shorts and a T-shirt, and then attacked her moving boxes with a vengeance. Her thoughts raced in a hundred different directions at once: the obstacles to starting her non-profit and how she'd overcome them, the lack of anything familiar in her life, trying to make her sister's home hers, Patrick — making her forget everything else.

She brushed her hair back from her damp forehead. Maybe coming here had been a colossal mistake. What had she been thinking? She'd sold her partnership in a successful business and her condo in Nashville, moved across the state to relocate in rural East Tennessee, where she knew no one. Well, no one except for Patrick, and that was more like having found someone she should avoid.

The doorbell rang, interrupting her jumbled thoughts. She looked up. Only an hour had ticked off the clock since her encounter with Patrick at the diner. How could that be? It felt like hours had passed.

Frannie approached the door hesitantly. Who would just drop by, unannounced, so late? Pushing back the lace curtain on the door, she found an attractive young woman with dark hair standing on the front porch. The woman smiled and lifted a hand in greeting. Frannie opened the door and tried to return the stranger's smile. She was beautiful, petite and shapely with long, thick hair and a lovely smooth, olive complexion.

"Hi. I'm Candi Heart." Juggling a large gift basket, she extended her hand, and Frannie took it automatically despite the shock that must have registered on her face. This was the woman involved in the scandal that Jenny had gotten tangled up in before going into witness protection.

"I'm sorry to come by so late and unannounced. I just closed up the shop, and thought I'd take a chance on finding you here on my way home," she said, her accent thick with the sound of the mountains.

Frannie retrieved her hand and rubbed it across her hip. Should she invite her in? Of course. Courtesy dictated she must. "Please, come in." She took a step back and made room for Candi to pass.

"I don't want to keep you, but I have a little welcome gift for you." With both hands, she lifted the large basket filled with a number of items. "I would have called, but I guess you haven't had a phone installed yet."

Frannie hadn't even thought about it. "I only have my cell," she said, opening the door wide. "Won't you come into the parlor?" She gestured toward the sitting room. There were boxes everywhere, some empty, some still taped, and others half unpacked, with the items that had been inside all over the place. She cleared off enough room for the two of them to sit on the sofa. "Sorry about the mess."

"No worries. You're just getting settled."

They both sat, facing each other. Candi smiled.

"You didn't have to go to all this trouble," Frannie said, looking at the heavy basket Candi held in her lap.

"Oh, we do this when newcomers relocate

here. Call it the Welcome Wagon, if you will. The mayor's wife used to do it, but I've taken over since she passed. I own a little women's shop in town where I sell a variety of things: flowers, candy, teas, clothing, perfumes and lotions. So, it seemed natural for me to volunteer for the job."

"I see." The mention of the mayor's deceased wife made Frannie even more uncomfortable. She hated the feeling of guilt and wondered if that would ever change. She sighed. Probably not.

"Can I be honest with you?" Candi asked.

Dear Lord. There was a lot of that going around. Frannie shrugged when what she really wanted to say was, *No, please just leave the basket and go.* She'd had about all the open and honest she could handle for one day.

No such luck.

"My coming to Angel Ridge was a difficult transition, for the town as well as for me. In such a small town, it can be unsettling for a time to the normal course of things when an outsider comes."

She moved the basket to the table in front of them and leaned toward Frannie. There was something about Candi. She radiated a deep calm that Frannie longed for, while *unsettled* was the word that described how she felt at the moment.

Candi's gaze surveyed the room. "When I moved to town, I didn't bring a lot of things with me. I wanted to start fresh, leave my old life behind."

Frannie wondered what that meant. It was Candi's past that had, as she had said, unsettled everyone, including Jenny, changing their family forever.

"But you bring things with you whether you pack them in boxes or carry them inside. In my case, some family ghosts lingered in Angel Ridge that I knew nothing about."

"Really?"

Candi nodded. "My mother had also left our mountain home to come to Angel Ridge, when she was about the same age as me. After she arrived, she chose a path that led to trouble and heartache. When she returned to her home on the mountain, she had me. But she brought her troubles home with her and died under mysterious circumstances. So, I was raised by a grandmother who tried to protect me from my mamma's truths — truths that were here waiting for me."

"I'm sorry," Frannie said, and she was. Sorry for Candi and for Jenny. They'd both gotten snared in a dead woman's haunting past.

"I'm so sorry your sister got tangled up in my family troubles," Candi said, as if she'd read Frannie's mind. "You must miss Jenny terribly."

All Frannie could do was nod. She felt the familiar tears clog her throat. What she wouldn't give to have her sister to talk to now. Candi reached out and squeezed Frannie's hand. The contact felt comforting and somehow familiar. When she looked into Candi's eyes, a little of the peace and calm that radiated from her stole into Frannie. She held Candi's hand with both of hers, closing her eyes to let the feeling settle some of the turmoil of the day.

"I know it seems unlikely, given the trouble I brought to your sister's life," Candi said, "but you and I have a soul-deep connection, the healing kind that springs from tragedy. It's the way of things. When you lose something precious, God sends help along to get you through." Candi squeezed her hands, and when their eyes met, she smiled. "I've been waiting for you to come. I'm so glad you're finally here."

"I don't understand."

Candi laughed — the kind of laugh that takes over the body and seeps out of every pore, so that everyone near feels it. She tipped her head back, closed her eyes and then looked heavenward. "Oh, honey, we waste so much time tryin' to understand, when what we really need to do is just be. I don't understand why my mamma got involved with the people she did. I don't understand why she died so young, and I never knew her. I don't understand why bad people try to hurt the ones we love. Truth be told, I don't want to understand that kind of evil. But I do know it all added up to me being who I am and my being here, right now, with you being who you are, here with me. Right here in this moment is where we're meant to be. Our only job is to live in the *now* of our lives."

"We can't change what's happened, but we can choose to go forward."

"That's right. We, all of us, were put here for a purpose. There's work that we need to be about. Work no one else can do, and if we don't do it, it won't get done. And that'd be a pure waste and a shame."

Leaning in, Frannie said, "I feel that so strongly. How did you know?"

"Don't think I'm crazy," Candi said, "but I come from a long line of women who knew things, things about life and healing and nurturing, and trusting instincts and intuition."

"Seers?"

"We were called a lot of things. More than a hundred years ago, on the mountain, we were called granny women. Outsiders called us witches, but there was never anything magical or mystical about our gifts."

"So, your mother and her mother . . ."

"And her mother. Yep. They passed it down from generation to generation."

"Even though you're no longer a part of that mountain culture?"

"It's inside me — the way I learned to be in the world," Candi said. "Our history is a part of us, whether we know about it or not. It affects those who lived it and the generations that follow. It's the same for you. You and Jenny were cut from the same cloth, though you chose different paths."

"Do you think so?" She'd always been so careful and conservative while Jenny never met a risk she wasn't willing to take.

"Isn't that why you're here?"

"Yes." Frannie wanted to use her skills to help people find a better life. She believed so strongly in the project that she'd left everything familiar to come to a place where her sister had paid a heavy price for doing the right thing. Frannie had thought being in Angel Ridge, where she could remember her sister's strength and resolve, would give her some of her sister's courage.

"There are going to be obstacles."

Frannie smiled, feeling her resolve renew inside her. "There always are."

"But when you're doing something you feel passionate about, things have a way of working out exactly the way they should. You just have to stay focused and realize that distractions are the Devil's design to lead you astray."

Right. And Patrick was the devil of a tempting distraction. She just needed to look at him in a different light, one that focused on the role he played here in the present rather than the mistake he'd been in her past.

Candi stood. "I'll let you get back to unpacking." Frannie walked her to the door. "I hope you'll stop by my shop for a cup of tea. I'd love to hear what you have planned for your life in Angel Ridge. I'm sure you're going to do something amazing that will leave its mark on our little town, and I know I'm going to want to be a part of it."

Miss Estelee had said practically the same thing. Impulsively, Frannie gave Candi a hug. "I hope you'll be part of it. You've helped me see things much more clearly." She leaned back and looked down at Candi.

"Thank you."

Tears filled Candi's eyes. "Thank you. If it wasn't for your sister, I wouldn't be here living my dream."

Frannie opened the door and watched Candi walk down the front steps, then out onto the sidewalk. She was an example of a life positively affected by Jenny's passion for revealing truth. As Frannie closed the door, she leaned against it and imagined a day when she would see a life transformed because of something she had done. This was why she'd come here, and she vowed to keep her focus securely on that goal.

CHAPTER 6

Patrick sat at the counter in Ferguson's enjoying a peaceful mid-morning break and a cup of coffee. Since Frannie Thompson had come to town, there had been non-stop people dropping into his office to express their feelings about her non-profit locating right on Main Street in Angel Ridge. The Town Hall Meeting she had planned couldn't come soon enough.

They hadn't spoken since their attempted business dinner. He'd apologized, albeit later than he should have, and had tried to establish a professional relationship with her. He had figured the best course of action for now would be to give her space, since attraction flared between them whenever they were together.

At some point, however, he needed to let her know about pressing issues concerning her house. Though he dreaded that conversation, it had to happen sooner rather than later.

Dixie pushed through the swinging door that separated the kitchen from the rest of the diner, interrupting his thoughts. She stepped behind the counter where he sat and picked up a cloth, swiping unnecessarily at the pristine surface. "So, to what do I owe the pleasure? You're not usually around this time of the morning."

Patrick sipped his coffee. "Hiding out."

"You? Avoiding your responsibilities? Imagine that."

He could always count on Dixie to give him hell. For some reason, that made him smile. Despite the fact their relationship hadn't been easy since he'd married Susan, he liked his wife's best friend a lot, always had. She'd been a rock during Susan's illness and had gone the extra mile with his kids since her passing.

"There should be a revolving door at my office. I needed a break."

"Let me guess. The new business opening up on Main?"

He set his cup down. "As usual, you have your finger on the pulse of the town."

"It's all anyone is talking about."

The front door opened, and Patrick's mother breezed into the diner. "Oh, good," she said. "You're here." She presented her cheek for his kiss before she sat. "I thought I saw you come into the diner. You are impossible to track down these days."

"I was just saying the same thing, Mrs. Houston. Patrick never seems to be where he should," Dixie said. "How are you this fine day?"

"I'm well, dear. You're looking lovely and colorful, as usual," his mother said, referring to Dixie's bright yellow ensemble.

"Yellow puts me in mind of colored eggs, and Easter is only a few weeks away."

"That it is. Will you be helping with the Easter egg hunt in Town Square again this year?"

"Wouldn't miss it," Dixie said. "You dressing up in the rabbit suit again, Patrick?"

He'd forgotten about that. Grimacing, he sipped his coffee, keeping quiet. Maybe if he didn't commit —

"Of course he is," his mother answered for him. "Wouldn't be Easter without an Easter Bunny."

Great. "There's your answer," Patrick said. "Can I get you anything, Mrs. Houston? Coffee? Some iced tea?"

"Oh, iced tea sounds lovely."

So much for his peace and quiet. Apparently his mother wanted to discuss something.

"I just brewed a fresh batch. Let me sweeten it, and I'll be right back," Dixie said, and then disappeared into the kitchen.

"I'm so glad I found you, Patrick. I wanted to ask you about Frannie Thompson."

"She does seem to be the topic of discussion these days," Patrick said.

"I couldn't help noticing that there seemed to be something between the two of you that night you were having dinner here at the diner."

"Frannie and I shared a business dinner to discuss her plans for starting a non-profit foundation here in town. That's all," Patrick said.

"You are speaking to your mother, Patrick Houston. You may be able to fool most, but not me. From where I sat, it seemed to be more than a business dinner."

Patrick kept quiet. It wouldn't do any good to speak until she'd gotten it all out, and he felt sure there was more.

"And after talking to her, I am certain that I am correct."

"You spoke to her?" Patrick said, his voice elevating in equal proportion to his panic.

"Yes, dear. I interviewed her for the *Chronicle*."

Oh, no. This couldn't be good. "What did you say?"

"I don't know what you mean."

Dixie came back out then, frustrating him. Now he wouldn't be able to ask his mother further questions until Dixie left.

"Here you go," Dixie said, setting the iced tea in front of his mother.

"Thank you, dear."

Dixie tipped her head toward Patrick. "So, what's he done now?"

"Oh, nothing, I'm afraid," Mrs. Houston said, a sadness lacing her words. "I was just telling Patrick that I interviewed that lovely Frannie Thompson for the paper."

"Do tell," Dixie said, crossing her arms and leaning a hip against the counter.

Great. Just great.

"Frannie tells me she's single."

"Mother . . ." Patrick warned.

"Really? I'm sure Patrick hasn't given the fair Ms. Thompson a second thought, he's been so busy," Dixie said, sarcasm dripping from her words.

"More's the pity," Mrs. Houston said.

Enough was enough. "Anything else you wanted to discuss, Mother?"

"Yes, as a matter of fact there is. I'd like to take the children for ice cream after school today."

107

"Sure. I'll text and ask them to meet you at your house."

"Thank you, dear. Dixie, if you'll just give me another moment to speak to my son?"

"Of course," Dixie said. "I'll go check on my pies."

With Dixie securely out of hearing range, Patrick turned and said, "Mom, I wish you hadn't implied the things you did about Frannie and me in front of Dixie. I hope you haven't said anything like that to others."

"Of course not," Mrs. Houston said. "Well . . . maybe your aunt."

"Mom!"

"Oh, Patrick. I'm sorry, but she's such a lovely young woman, and seeing the two of you together and the interest you showed her, well, it gave me hope that you might be ready to move on." She patted his hand. "It's time, dear."

He couldn't dispute that, but he also didn't need her matchmaking. "Mom, I appreciate your concern, but if I decide to date again, it'll be my decision as to who and when."

"I'm sorry if I've upset you." She touched his cheek. "I worry about you, dear."

He took her hand and kissed it. "I'm fine, Mom. Really."

"Forgive an old woman her meddling? I forget myself sometimes."

"There's nothing to forgive. I love you."

Her eyes misted. "I love you, too, darling boy. You've been the joy of my life."

Squeezing her hand, Patrick said, "Hey, what's all this?" He handed her a napkin, and she dabbed at her eyes.

"I just want to see you happy before . . . well, I'm not going to be around forever."

"Is something wrong?" Patrick asked, concerned.

"No, no. I'm just feeling sentimental. You know, it's almost my anniversary."

He'd forgotten. Patrick's parents had shared a true and enduring love until his dad had died fifteen years ago. His mother hadn't even considered remarrying. She couldn't imagine loving anyone like that again. Witnessing their love up close had set off a longing in him for the same.

"I'm sorry," he said to his mother. "I'd forgotten about your anniversary."

A faraway look clouded her eyes. "I never will."

Patrick sat there, holding her hand, offering what comfort he could. But he was a poor substitute for the love of her life.

After a few moments ticked by, his mother said with a smile, "Well, I should go."

"Are you sure you're all right?" Patrick asked.

His mother stood. "Of course." She kissed his cheek and looked into his eyes. "So like your father," she said. "You deserve to be happy. I wish you believed that."

"I am happy, Mom."

Her smile looked so sad now. "Of course you are. Goodbye, dear. I'll have the children home before dinner."

Patrick nodded, and she was gone, leaving him feeling gutted and wanting to fill the gaping wound. Before, he would have buried the feeling at the bottom of a bottle. Now, he just had to endure the pain.

"Looks like you've got a matchmaker on your hands," Dixie said.

Patrick turned, surprised. He hadn't heard her walk up. "She means well." He picked up a napkin and started shredding it. He needed to focus on something else, and seeing Dixie made him think of his daughter. "Dix, if you're not too busy, would you mind talking about Abby for a minute?"

"I'm always happy to talk about my godchildren," Dixie said.

"She's been distant lately. I can't get her to talk to me at all."

"She's a teenage girl. I'd call that normal behavior."

"I'm worried about her. She's been dressing strangely, spending a lot of time on the Internet and texting."

"Normal," Dixie repeated. "Her grades are fine, and she does a good job here. Shows up on time and works hard. Just be there for her, Patrick, and when she decides to talk, she'll know you're *available*." She emphasized the last word, subtly reminding him of all the years he hadn't been available to anyone in his life.

"Does she talk to you . . . about her mom?"

"Not a lot. But she goes with me every Tuesday to put flowers on Susan's grave."

Tuesday. Susan had died on a Tuesday.

He hadn't been to the cemetery since the graveside service.

"It's nice that she can do that with you," he said softly. He looked down at his coffee to hide the emotion that must show clearly in his eyes.

Dixie squeezed his hand, surprising him with the uncharacteristic expression of comfort. "The kids can always count on me."

He smiled, placing his other hand on top of hers. "Thank you."

Dixie nodded, then pulled her hand away

and swiped at the counter. "Can I get you a refill?"

"No, thanks." He pulled a couple of dollars out of his pocket and put them on the counter. "I need to get back."

"You haven't said what you think about Frannie Thompson's plan."

He crossed his arms. "I think there are a few wrinkles to be worked out, but overall, I believe it'll be good for the town. What do you think about it?"

"Well, of course, I'm happy to have another female-run business in town. At this rate, it won't be long before the ladies take over and start running this place, as the good Lord intended. We have a woman doctor, a woman running the library, me and Candi operating successful businesses."

Patrick chuckled. "Should I be worried about my job?"

Dixie shrugged. "I'm just not sure about this one."

"What? Frannie or the business?"

"I think the non-profit will be a good thing for everyone. Should help a lot of people get back on their feet in this economy."

Patrick nodded. "I'm sensing a 'but' coming."

"It's Frannie. Don't you think it's weird?

Her being here after all that went down with her sister? I mean, things have been so calm for years now, but her coming to town is going to remind everyone of all the bad things that happened after Candi came to town."

"Candi never left. She's the one who should be the reminder. With her here, there's always the possibility that trouble could come looking for her again."

"But it hasn't."

"Right. Jenny's gone instead. I think Frannie just wants a fresh start in a place her sister loved."

Dixie crossed her arms and leaned a hip against the counter. "And you make that opinion based on what? Have you been seeing her?"

"Not you, too," he grumbled. Women and their need to know everything. "Ours is a business relationship."

"And that's it? Strictly business?"

"Yes, but even if it wasn't, I can't see how it's anyone's business but mine and Frannie's," he said firmly.

"The truth comes out. You are interested in her."

He sighed. "Say your piece." She would anyway, even without his invitation.

"I get the impression something happened

between the two of you," Dixie said. "She has always been decidedly uncomfortable around you."

Patrick was not about to spill his guts about his indiscretion with Frannie. Sharing that bit of knowledge with anyone would serve absolutely no purpose. He certainly didn't want to make things worse for Frannie. Dixie's good opinion, once lost, was impossible to regain. So, he decided to turn the tables.

"Maybe she's attracted to me."

"Please." Dixie huffed and rolled her eyes.

"I know you find it hard to believe, but it's not impossible that someone would find me attractive. Susan did."

"I never understood that either," Dixie said flatly. "No. It's more likely you've thrown some unwelcome advances her way."

"What if I am interested in her? Would that be so terrible?" Patrick said quietly. "I don't plan to spend the rest of my life alone, Dixie."

"And no one's saying you should, but I can't help feeling that there's more to the story where Frannie's concerned."

The bells on the door jangled, announcing another customer and saving Patrick from having to reply.

He turned to see Frannie walk through

the door. The conversation about moving on and attraction had him reacting to her in spite of himself. She looked stunning in a soft pink pantsuit that brought out the red highlights in her dark hair. The short jacket drew his attention to her long legs and shapely backside. He sucked in a deep breath and pulled back on the reins of that line of thinking, but everything about her appealed to him. His mind told him she was off-limits, but his body had other ideas, vivid ideas that had played out in more than a few of his recent dreams.

"Speak of the devil," Dixie said. "The Mayor and I were just talking about you."

Patrick whipped his gaze back to Dixie.

"Really?" Frannie said. "Anything I should know about?"

Not waiting for Dixie to respond, Patrick said, "I was saying that I'll be glad when you hold the Town Hall Meeting. All I seem to get done is fielding questions and concerns about your business plan."

Dixie added, "We both think what you want to do will be good for Angel Ridge."

"Thank you. The Town Hall Meeting is actually why I'm here, Dixie. I wanted to order refreshments for the event. I should have come by sooner, but I've been so busy with the renovations, setting up the office, and settling into my house. It's only a couple of days away. I hope you can do it."

"What did you have in mind?"

"Nothing elaborate. Water, coffee, lemonade and maybe some small cookies?"

"Shouldn't be a problem. Do you need wait staff or will you have someone there who can handle refills when things get low?"

"My assistant will be there, but she'll be up front helping me with the presentation. Actually, you know, your mother came by asking if I needed volunteer help for anything. Maybe she would be available."

"I'm sure she'd be glad to," Dixie said. "I'll ask her. My guess is most of the town will be there, so the diner will probably be deserted."

"I'm sorry about that," Frannie said.

"No worries," Dixie said. "This is big news and something the entire town will want to hear about."

"Thank you for the support. I appreciate it."

"It's a good program. I look forward to being involved," Dixie said. "I'll work up a quote and send it to your office this afternoon."

"Excellent."

"If you'll both excuse me, I have pies in the oven that need to come out."

After Dixie disappeared into the kitchen, an awkward moment passed with neither Patrick nor Frannie knowing what to do or say. The silence had him wondering what it would be like if they went out on a real date. Could she leave the situation surrounding their first meeting behind? Her gaze slid down his body, and he felt that quick look all the way to his toes. The attraction was definitely there. Maybe she could be persuaded.

A man on crutches, struggling to open the door and maneuver his way inside the diner interrupted his thoughts. Patrick moved quickly to hold the door and got quite a shock when he saw who it was.

"Thanks, man."

"Jonathan. I didn't know you were in town . . . and injured. What happened?"

Jonathan Temple had grown up in Angel Ridge. He was a former Angel Ridge High football star and University of Tennessee standout who'd made it to the pros. As a fullback, he hadn't made a big splash, but he'd enjoyed a long, successful career since leaving Tennessee. The great Jonathan Temple had it all: looks, a personality that drew people to him and athletic ability that had taken him far. But he'd left a mess behind when he'd moved out of Angel

Ridge. Patrick, for one, had hoped he would continue to stay away, but he'd blown in and out of town before. Hopefully, this would be another one of those times.

"Knee injuries. I've had several over the years," Jonathan said as he came in and made straight for a stool at the counter. "And on top of that, I tore pretty much everything there was to tear in my knee playing basketball, of all things, and messed up all the repairs from previous surgeries. Long story short, since I can rehab anywhere, I thought why not come home? Nothing like spring in East Tennessee, right?"

Patrick did not like where this was going. And what was he doing in the diner? Dixie didn't need to get messed up with this guy again.

Looking at Frannie, Jonathan extended a hand. "Hi, I'm Jonathan Temple. Forgive me for not standing."

And there was that charming smile. Some things didn't change.

Frannie came forward and offered Jonathan her hand. "Frannie Thompson."

Jonathan took her hand and held it. "You must be new in town, because I'm certain I'd remember such a beautiful woman."

Patrick gave Jonathan a look, but he

missed it because Frannie had his complete attention.

"Frannie just moved to Angel Ridge," Patrick said. "She's developing the empty buildings on Main and starting a non-profit."

"Really? Intersting. I'd like to hear more about it."

"We're having a Town Hall Meeting to discuss it Thursday evening at the court-house," Frannie said. "Everyone's invited, so you should come."

Patrick didn't miss that she'd said "every-one" was invited, so it didn't seem as if she was issuing Jonathan a personal invitation. Patrick couldn't help smiling, appreciating Frannie even more, if that were possible.

"The only thing on my calendar for the foreseeable future is therapy, and that's dur-ing the day. So I'll welcome the distraction, even though I'm no longer officially a resident of Angel Ridge."

"Did I hear the door?" Dixie called from the back.

Jonathan put his finger to his lips, then pointed to himself, silently asking that no one tip off who had come in. Patrick took a step forward, his intent to warn Jonathan off, but Dixie pushed through the swinging door and skidded to a stop when she saw him.

"Hello, Austin," he said, referring to the town where Dixie had been born.

Dixie, to her credit, only let her emotions show for a split second before moving forward with her characteristic confidence and spunk. "Look what the cat dragged in. Jonathan Temple."

"I'm here with my hat in my hand," Jonathan said.

In response, Dixie simply lifted her eyebrows, looking for all the world as if she could care less what the man did with his hat. Good girl.

"I had knee surgery."

"I heard," Dixie said.

"Really?"

She shrugged. "I do read, and the Knoxville paper so enjoys printing whatever tidbit they can about you."

"Once a Vol, always a Vol," he said referring to the mascot of the University of Tennessee. "I decided to come home to rehab."

"By home, I presume you mean Knoxville, since you haven't called Angel Ridge home since high school," Patrick interjected.

"Actually, I'll be staying here in Angel Ridge."

"Until training camp opens for the Seahawks this summer?" Patrick asked.

Jonathan gave Patrick a steady look. Or should he call that a challenging look? "I'm afraid my playing days are over. I'm back, for good."

Frannie and Dixie had become spectators in Patrick's and Jonathan's back and forth conversation. Patrick tried to gauge Dixie's reaction to this unexpected bit of news. She was looking at Jonathan like he'd grown a second head.

Frannie bowed out first. "If you'll excuse me, I need to get back to work. Jonathan, it was nice to meet you. Dixie, thank you for your help with the refreshments."

"Sure thing," Dixie said, but didn't take her gaze from Jonathan, who was beginning to squirm under her scrutiny.

Frannie spared Patrick a brief glance, then turned and left. They really needed to have a private conversation, but with Jonathan turning up, now was not the time. Maybe Patrick would drop by her house later tonight. He rubbed his jaw. Probably not the best idea, but . . .

"So, you think you can stroll back into town after being gone all these years and act like nothing has changed?" Dixie asked.

He lifted his steel crutches. "I wouldn't call what I'm doing strolling."

121

"You know what I mean."

"I know my being here is a little awkward and possibly disrupting —"

"That would make you the master of understatement," Dixie said.

"But I think it's time I came home."

Jonathan glanced at Patrick who wanted nothing more than to bury his fist in Jonathan's face, something he would have done years ago if Jonathan had been around. But anger was the precursor to his wanting a drink, so he took a breath and did his best to quell his rising temper.

"Why?" Dixie asked. "Why do you suddenly need to come back to Hicktown USA when you have a palatial estate complete with a Barbie doll wife in Seattle?"

"*Barbara* and I are divorced. It was final last week."

Dixie folded her arms, but didn't comment.

"What? The *News-Sentinel* didn't pick up that story?" Jonathan asked.

"No. They also didn't pick up that your career was over, which I frankly find surprising," Dixie said.

"I just found out myself. When the doctors got in there to do the repairs, they were uncertain about my chances for playing again. After several months of therapy, it's become clear that I won't be able to go back. The Seahawks will do the press releases later in the week."

Patrick pulled in a deep breath. "Great. Just what we need. Press swarming all over town trying to get a statement from you while everybody's in an uproar over Frannie Thompson's non-profit."

"An uproar over a non-profit?" Jonathan said.

"You know the old guard gets their knickers in a wad over anything new," Dixie said, "especially if it wasn't their idea. Oh, sorry. I forgot. You've been away so long, you wouldn't remember how things work around here anymore."

"Where are you staying?" Patrick asked.

"Years ago, I bought the old Jones place at the end of Ridge Road."

"That old place?" Dixie said. "That eye sore's been about to fall down for ages, but Mrs. McKay wouldn't hear of letting such 'an historic landmark be destroyed,' " she said, the last in a fair imitation of the town matriarch.

"I always loved that old place," Jonathan said. "Cole and Blake had a look at it, and both believe that a restoration is possible."

"Good Lord . . ." Dixie breathed. "My own brother knew this and didn't tell me."

She picked up the wet cloth she'd used to wipe the counter, then threw it back down. Cocking a hand on her hip, she said, "What do you want, Temple? And bear in mind that I damn well don't care where you hang your hat."

"I need your help."

The man was unbelievable. Given their history, Jonathan had no right to impose on Dixie. Patrick stood back and watched the fireworks display that was sure to ensue.

"You've got some nerve, Temple, coming here and asking me for anything." Dixie's voice was low and laced with anger, the kind that was deep-seated and had been simmering for years.

Foolishly ignoring that, Jonathan forged ahead. "Blake and Cole have the water working, so I have a kitchen and bathroom, but the kitchen isn't functional. Not that I could do much with my leg in this brace." He swept a hand across the black brace he wore that extended from ankle to thigh. "I need someone to bring in meals."

"And you thought I'd jump at the opportunity to spend time with you?"

"Since I've been away so long, I didn't know who else to ask."

"Well then," Dixie said, "I guess you're stuck between the proverbial rock and a hard place. Guess which one I am?"

"Take my pick?" Jonathan hazarded.

"Smart man."

"Careful. That halfway passes as a compliment." His smile was designed to charm and disarm. It didn't work.

"You would be incorrect."

"Come on, Dix," Jonathan pleaded.

"She said 'no,' " Patrick interjected.

Dixie lifted a hand. "I am perfectly capable of handling this."

Patrick held up his hands and took a step back, but didn't leave. He had a few words for Temple when Dixie was through with him.

Dixie braced her hands on the counter and leaned in toward Jonathan. "First of all, before you decided to relocate to Angel Ridge, you should have considered what kind of a reception you would receive when you got here. Regardless of whether my brother, Blake, and the rest of this town would welcome you back with open arms, you should not expect that the same sentiment extends to me. Second, if you need help with anything, do not expect that it will be forthcoming from this quarter. And third," she lowered her voice and moved in closer, "you have some nerve waltzing in here like we're friends and I'd consider doing *anything* for you."

Jonathan teased the dragon and leaned in as well.

Patrick took a step closer, ready to step in if it came to blows. Not that Jonathan would raise a hand to Dixie, but he couldn't say the same for her when it came to Jonathan. When he'd gotten out of East Tennessee to play pro football, one of the numerous offenses he'd left in his wake was brutally breaking Dixie's heart. And to add insult to injury, he'd almost immediately married someone else.

"I know I don't deserve your forgiveness, but I'm asking for it anyway. I hope we can all," Jonathan said, glancing back at Patrick, "get past what happened all those years ago."

"And what? Be friends?" Dixie said. "Not likely."

"It was a long time ago, Dix. We were just kids."

"Poor behavior speaks to character."

"Circumstances change people," Jonathan said softly.

"Older and wiser and all that garbage? Forgive me, but I'll need to see it to believe it. Now, if you'll excuse me, I have work to do."

She turned and went back into the

kitchen, leaving Patrick alone with Jonathan.

Patrick wasted no time. "You can't be serious about moving back here."

"It's done," he said flatly.

"Your being here is completely unacceptable. How could you think this was a good idea?"

"I need to make things right."

This was hitting way too close to home. If anyone understood needing to make amends for past wrongs, it was Patrick.

"The truth has to come out sometime. It's been like a cancer eating away at both of us."

Patrick's jaw locked against the emotion he felt at hearing the word "cancer."

Jonathan closed his eyes. "You know what I mean," he said softly. "I hurt everyone I loved, and kept hurting them with the choices I made. Secrets eat away at everything good inside you until all that's left is bad," Jonathan finished softly. "I just want to find the good again."

"At what expense?" Patrick said just as softly. "Haven't we paid enough?"

CHAPTER 7

Frannie knocked off work around four.

She had gotten so much accomplished in these last weeks. Blake Ferguson and his crew had finished work on the Foundation offices. At Candi's recommendation, she'd hired Candi's Aunt Verdi as her administrative assistant. A former teacher and lifelong resident of Angel Ridge, her assistance had been invaluable. Frannie had also had some volunteer assistance from Dixie's and Blake's mother, who had been helpful with posting fliers and preparing mailings.

But with the Town Hall Meeting only a few days away, Frannie had decided to come home to dig weeds from her overgrown flowerbeds while she thought about her presentation. It was mindless work that needed doing and would allow her to think about possible questions from the townspeople.

She didn't know how long she'd been at it

when a young boy appeared without her noticing his approach. "Hidee," he said.

"Hello." Frannie shaded her eyes from the setting sun and squinted at the boy. Tall and lanky, he had golden red curls and freckles, and looked to be somewhere between ten and twelve.

"My name's Sammy. I'm your next door neighbor." He thumbed toward the house next to hers. "I knowed somebody moved into Miss Jenny's house, but I hadn't seen you 'til now."

Frannie stood and removed her gardening gloves so she could shake the boy's hand. "I'm pleased to meet you, Sammy. My name is Frannie."

His smile was huge and engaging. "Frannie. That sounds kinda like Jenny, but you don't look so much like her. She didn't have dark hair."

"Jenny was my sister," Frannie said. "Our mamma liked that our names sounded alike."

"You're Miss Jenny's sister?"

"I sure am."

"I was sorry when she died in that explosion. She was so nice. She'd have me and my sister over to watch movies. But sometimes it was just me, because my sister wouldn't want to come. Miss Jenny'd make

129

popcorn, and ever now and then, we'd have ice cream, too."

"Jenny loved ice cream. I bet it was chocolate."

"It sure was," Sammy agreed, nodding his head. "You must be missing her something awful, her being your sister and all."

"Yes. I do."

He continued to nod, his expression solemn. "I understand. My mamma died a couple of years ago."

"I'm so sorry," Frannie said. A boy this young shouldn't have had to deal with that much loss. First his neighbor and then his mom. How awful for him.

"So, you're living in Miss Jenny's house. That's nice. I'm glad to have a neighbor again."

Frannie smiled. "Thank you."

"I noticed that your grass is gettin' high."

Frannie stood on protesting knees. She'd knelt too long. "Yes. My sister's mower won't start, and I haven't had a chance to take it to be repaired." Not that she'd know where to take it, but she thought she'd ask at the hardware store when she had a chance.

"I'd be glad to cut it for you. My daddy said when I got to be in the fifth grade, I could mow yards to earn extra money. I'm in the fourth grade now, but I'll be a fifth grader in just a few months, so I don't think he'd mind me starting early, especially since you're just right next door."

She'd be glad to let him mow her yard, but felt this enterprising young man should be treated as anyone else asking to mow her yard. "That might just work for me. How much would you charge?"

"Well, I was figurin' to charge folks twenty-five dollars, but bein' as you're my next door neighbor and all, I'd make you a good deal and only charge you fifteen."

"That's very neighborly of you, Sammy. I'd be happy to have you cut my grass. I don't really have time to tend to it right now, anyway."

"And besides that, your mower's not working," Sammy added.

She laughed. He was sharp. "That's right."

"I might could get to it tomorrow, if my daddy says it's okay."

"Tomorrow's fine," Frannie said. She shaded her eyes again when she saw the mayor coming up her walk. Great. What was he doing here? As he drew closer, she noticed he looked more rumpled than usual. In fact, he looked a little gray, like he wasn't feeling well.

"What's up?" Patrick said with a strained smile.

Sammy turned, a huge grin transforming his face. "Hey, Daddy. I was just meeting our new neighbor. Her name's Frannie. She's Miss Jenny's sister who used to live here. Frannie, this is my daddy. He's the mayor."

Dear Lord! She lived next door to Patrick? *Had* been living next door to him all these weeks and hadn't known it?

Patrick put his arm around his son's shoulders. "Ms. Thompson and I have met, sport. What were you two talking about?" To Frannie, he said, "I hope he wasn't troubling you."

Something was definitely off with Patrick. He seemed . . . lifeless. Drained. "No, of course not. He was just offering to help me out by mowing my yard."

"Yeah, Daddy, and I'm only charging her fifteen dollars. Ain't that bein' neighborly?"

Patrick smiled down at his son as he squeezed his shoulder. "*Isn't,* and yes, that is being neighborly, but aren't you jumping the gun, sport?"

"There's only two more months left of the fourth grade, and then I'll be a fifth grader. I'm the same age now as I'm gonna be this summer, and people's grass needs mowin' now. And besides, Frannie's mower don't work."

"Doesn't." Patrick laughed, smoothing his son's red curls. The boy's face flushed with embarrassment, and he moved away from his father's touch. That seemed to pain Patrick as well, watching his child pull away because he felt too old to have his hair ruffled by his father.

Patrick shifted his gaze to her. "I'd be glad to take a look at your mower."

"Oh, no. That's all right. I'll check with Mr. DeFoe to see if he can recommend someone to come by and have a look at it for me."

"It's no trouble. It's been sitting for some time now. The gas line probably needs to be flushed and the oil changed."

"Or I could mow it for her if you'll let me," Sammy said, a hopeful look in his green eyes.

"How about we talk about it later?" Patrick said.

The boy's face fell. He looked down and kicked at a clump of grass with the toe of his sneaker. "All right."

"Why don't you run on inside and get your homework out so I can check it," Patrick said. "I'll be along in a minute."

"Okay. Nice to meet you, Miss Frannie.

I'm really happy we're gonna be neighbors."

And before she knew what was happening, he threw his arms around her waist, gave her a hug, and then just as quickly, he was gone, running toward his house and in through the back door.

"Sorry about that," Patrick said. He was looking at her flowerbed rather than her.

"Don't be. Your son is charming," she said.

"Yes," Patrick agreed. "He's a great kid," he said, still not looking at her.

"Did you send him over to pave the way to letting me know that we live next door to each other, since you couldn't manage it yourself?"

He looked at her then. "Wow, you see me as quite the villain."

"It's no secret that I don't have a favorable impression of you. Case in point, the fact that you failed to let me know that you live next door."

"I was just coming over to correct that, but unfortunately, my son beat me to it."

"Right. Why didn't you tell me sooner?" Frannie asked.

He looked away, then back at her. When he spoke, his words were hard, clipped. "We haven't talked about anything other than business for weeks. That's how you wanted it."

It had not escaped her notice that he'd left her alone in the past weeks. She'd wondered if he'd done it on purpose. "So, it was one more thing to add to a growing list of problems between the two of us," she said.

"I figured you were dealing with enough, and given our previous encounters, I didn't expect you to react well to the news." He slid his hands into his back pockets. "I'd say I was right."

She didn't need Patrick or anyone else looking after her. Crossing her arms, she said, "I suppose I should thank you then, for your concern about my stress level, and also for the control of information."

He sighed and focused on something behind her. Again, it struck her that he looked tired, run down, and thin. And here she was giving him hell. She almost felt bad about it. That surprised her.

"I don't want to argue," he said softly, still not looking at her. "I also don't want to upset you further, but I really can't do anything about the fact that I live next door."

Frannie nodded. Truth be told, she didn't want to argue either. Didn't want to lose her focus. There was something about the man that brought out the worst in her. She didn't typically respond to people this way, but he stirred so much emotion in her. That was the trouble. Sure, there had been men in her life, but never anyone who made her feel so much anger, and at the same time, so much desire.

At length, Frannie conceded, "Of course, you're right. I mean, I suppose I should have assumed that you lived nearby. It's a small town, after all."

That seemed to catch him off guard. He looked at her, surprised. "Yes. Actually, it's a wonder we haven't run into each other coming and going."

"I guess we keep different hours."

Patrick looked out at the river that stretched in front of the house. "Didn't you ever visit your sister?"

"No. I was in college when she moved here, and then got too busy building an interior design business." Frannie smiled, remembering. "We clocked a lot of cell phone hours." She'd been so angry and upset with Jenny when she'd left Nashville. Angel Ridge had seemed like the other end of the world, at the time. Now, Frannie would take a few hundred miles any day over never seeing her sister again.

Frannie rubbed her forehead, wishing that could clear her thoughts. "Just because we live next door to each other doesn't mean we have to interact. We can each keep to our respective sides of the fence."

"Or we could try something radical and make an effort to get along. We are neighbors after all. Now that you've opened your office, we're going to see a lot of each other, here and in town."

The idea had merit. It was exhausting having her guard up around him all the time and acting hateful when it wasn't in her nature. They didn't have to be best friends to be civil to each other. In fact, the thought of any kind of friendship between them left her feeling flat. They'd never manage being just friends.

Still, she found herself saying, "All right."

He swayed toward her, and she automatically reached out to steady him.

"Sorry. I'm feeling a little dizzy all of a sudden."

"Sit," she insisted, leading him over to her front steps. "Is something wrong? Are you ill?" And then it hit her. He was an alcoholic. She sniffed, but didn't smell anything. Still, she had to ask. "Patrick, have you been drinking?" she said softly.

"No! Of course not," he insisted. "I haven't eaten. I worked right through lunch and the afternoon, and then I had a meeting in Knoxville. It was so late, I decided to come straight home to grab something here."

"But you came to my house first because you saw Sammy in the yard." She nodded. "Let me get you a banana."

When she stepped past him, he grabbed her hand. "That's not necessary."

"I can't have you passing out on my front steps. Be still. I'll be right back."

Inside, Frannie decided to get him a glass of milk as well.

"Did I hear you right?" he said from behind her. "Did you just agree to try and tolerate me?"

Frannie dropped the milk she'd been holding into the sink mid-pour. It spilled everywhere, but Patrick reached around her and righted the carton. The movement had his body pressed up against hers, trapping her between him and the counter. Awareness exploded through her body.

Picking up a kitchen towel, she swiped at the liquid splattered on the counter and her T-shirt. "You startled me," she finally managed. She hadn't invited him in, and she didn't miss the fact that they were alone in her kitchen.

"Sorry."

He pulled her ponytail back over her

shoulder, exposing her neck and reminding her again of that blasted hazy memory of the kiss they'd shared all those years ago.

"Patrick . . . you shouldn't be here."

"I know, but I can't seem to help myself where you're concerned. Seeing you in town, knowing you're here in your house when I'm in mine," he sighed. "I can't stop thinking about you."

Patrick squeezed her arms and rested his forehead against hers.

Frannie closed her eyes, seeing snapshots of his lips on her neck, her face, her mouth. The memories were disjointed and vague because of the alcohol, but her body remembered. The intense feelings were the same.

"Do you think about me?" he whispered, those lips brushing her ear.

Frannie had to grab the counter to stay upright. Keeping busy had left little time for her mind to wander, but when she was in bed trying to fall asleep, thoughts of him had given her more than a few restless nights. Arguing with herself and recounting all the reasons she should erase Patrick from her mind had proven useless. Now, with him standing so close, touching her, stirring cloudy emotions and memories that could be replaced with vivid new ones, had her thinking she needed to step away from him.

But then his lips touched her neck, and she froze.

A featherlike touch trailing up her back lit up every nerve ending in her body. "The pull between us is so strong," he said against her neck. "Do you feel it?" He cupped her shoulders and pulled her back against him.

"We shouldn't," she said, but tilted her head to give him better access.

"Why?"

All the reasons flashed across her mind. He'd been married the first time they'd kissed, and even though he wasn't married now, she couldn't forget it. More importantly, she could not allow any distractions to cause her to lose focus on the non-profit at this critical time. But with him holding her and trailing soft kisses across her cheek, the temptation to turn her head fed a wicked desire to know what it would be like to be kissed by Patrick with her head clear. But did she dare go there? What would happen if she did? Maybe it would help get him out of her system. It couldn't be as amazing as her fuzzy, surely embellished memory, told her it had been.

She turned and rested her hands on his chest as he pulled her close. Their lips, so tantalizingly close, but not touching, made anticipation almost unbearable. He brought a hand up to cup her cheek while his gaze swept her features as if he were seeing them for the first time.

"So beautiful," he said softly.

No. Not beautiful. Jenny had been the beautiful sister. Frannie had been forgettable. But being on the receiving end of Patrick's intense silver gaze had her almost believing him.

"I wish we could start over. Pretend we just met."

Frannie had never been good at playing pretend. For her, reality always seemed to be waiting just around the corner. But for now, maybe she could stop time long enough to imagine.

"And if we could?" she asked.

The backs of his fingers trailed down her cheek and then her neck. "I'd ask you out. A quiet dinner at an out of the way restaurant in Knoxville, a chilled bottle of wine, for you." He smiled. "We could share some appetizers, have a chocolate dessert, dance to some laid back jazz, more wine."

She touched his face. Dark stubble teased her fingertips as she traced the line of his jaw, then lingered at his lower lip. "I wouldn't drink, knowing it's a problem for you."

"Since we're pretending, we could also

pretend it's not an issue."

"Sounds lovely." And it did. Like a fantasy that had her giving in and pressing her lips to his, so soft and warm, but then passion from her hazy memories blazed into Technicolor reality. He took control, tilted his head and kissed her slow, exploring by touching his tongue to hers and then retreating, each time returning to deepen the kiss. She'd never experienced anything like this. He didn't devour her or press or try to overpower her like so many men did. In fact, she had every opportunity to break the contact, but she wrapped her arms around his neck, wanting more. She'd never felt so desired, so cherished, so safe.

Patrick surprised her by breaking the kiss and pulling back a little. "There's no reason why we can't."

"Can't what?" She frowned, not completely understanding why they were no longer kissing, wishing they could get back to that amazing exploration that needed no words.

"Start over."

Frannie pressed her hands against his chest, and he took a step back, allowing her to move away from him. Maybe distance would allow her to think more clearly. She smoothed a hand over her head, pushing a

fallen strand of hair back toward her ponytail. Beautiful indeed. She was a mess.

"I didn't come to Angel Ridge with any
intention of finding you and picking up
where we left off," Frannie said. "I didn't
even know who you were. Wasn't sure if you
lived here."

"Even after the next morning in the diner
when we saw each other?"

"You could have moved. I didn't know
you were the mayor."

Ignoring that, Patrick said, "So you did
think about it? The kiss we shared?"

Of course she had, but she'd never admit
it. "Dating or having a relationship of any
kind is not in my plans."

Patrick smiled a slow, sexy smile and approached her, invading her space with his
scent, his smile, his warmth and all that
prickly awareness that always came with
him. "I'm not asking you to go steady."

She didn't know what she'd expected him
to say, but that threw her off balance, and
she laughed. How could he be joking? And
why was she responding to him?

"Then what are you asking?" she said.

He eased his arms around her and pulled
her up against him, holding her close and
tight. She couldn't help wrapping her arms
around him, too. It felt so good to just be

held. It had been so long since there'd been anyone in her life to offer affection or comfort. Keeping busy only got her so far. The long, lonely nights always found her, making her doubt that she could do it all on her own. Jenny had been so strong, had gone it alone for years. But in the end, even Jenny had found that she wanted, and maybe even had needed, to share her life with someone.

Dear Lord, she was treading dangerous ground here.

"Why are you doing this?" she asked, unable and unwilling to pull away now.

"Because you need this as much as I do."

Had he read her mind, or had she said something out loud without realizing she'd spoken? "You seem so sure. How can you know that?"

He cupped the back of her head and looked into her eyes for a long, breathless moment. "Our minds, our words, tell us all the reasons why we shouldn't, but our bodies tell the truth. We have an elemental need to be close to someone. That need usually wins out in the end, or we die lonely." His eyes filled with emotion. "I don't want to be lonely anymore."

Frannie felt herself falling, but she held out. "Why me?"

"Because," he paused, measuring his words. "I've been dead inside for so long. Somehow, you've brought me back to life. For the first time in a long time I want to feel everything instead of just wanting to feel numb."

She remembered him saying something about finding any reason to drink. Numbing the pain was one reason, she supposed. But now that he was sober, it must be hard to have no buffer from all the sensations coming at him. She knew about that, but rather than numb her pain with alcohol or some other substance, she withdrew so no one could see how she truly felt. It was bad enough she punished herself; no need in punishing everyone around her. She could put on her work face and get through the day, but when she came home, she locked herself inside and hid from the world, from life.

And now, here stood Patrick, beautiful, tortured Patrick, tempting her to share herself with him. Could they find peace with each other? Was that possible? Would it be worth the risks to find out if she could allow herself to feel everything, too?

Finally, she managed to say, "I don't know."

"What's holding you back?"

The familiar fear that went along with taking a risk came over Frannie. Alone was something she knew. Something she could be comfortable with. First there'd been the normal childhood with two parents she never got, then the isolation of her illness with others her age treating her like she was contagious. Jenny had been the only person Frannie had let get close, but in the end, she'd lost Jenny too.

She'd been locked up tight since Jenny had left. If Frannie gave in, even a little, and allowed herself to open up to this man, surely she'd be lost. It had taken all these years, but she'd just made it back to functioning — functioning alone. She couldn't risk a setback.

Tears stung the back of her eyes. She couldn't let him see her cry, so she pressed against his shoulders. "You should go."

Patrick put his hands on his hips and took a step back, leaving her cold and missing his warmth. "Okay," he said. He looked at her, a hard, searching look that surely saw straight to her soul. Could he see her wavering resolve? Reaching out, he touched the side of her face so tenderly, she nearly lost control.

"I can see that you want to, but something's holding you back — something more

146

than what happened between us in that bar. That's just an excuse to keep me at a distance. I know because I've been to hell and lived through it despite the God-awful pain the journey caused. When you've gone through something devastating, you can spot it when someone else has, too."

Her breath caught, and the tears were closer. She turned so he wouldn't see. "Please," she choked out. "Just go."

He squeezed her shoulders. Biting her lip, Frannie closed her eyes against the long suppressed emotions that now bubbled to the surface.

"I know I'm in no position to offer, but please, let me help."

"How?" she whispered.

He wrapped his arms around her waist and pulled her back against him. "Let me in."

The words "I can't" lodged in her throat, refusing to come out. So, she just shook her head from side to side, her eyes shut tight.

"You can't keep so much emotion locked up inside. It's destructive. The people you love wouldn't want you to hurt yourself that way."

There's no one, she thought, unable to say the words.

"You don't have to be alone. *We* don't

have to be alone."

Her breathing was fast and shallow, the precursor to the hyperventilation that came with the panic attacks.

"Breathe," he whispered in her ear, his hand making soothing circles on her stomach. "It's okay."

It would never be okay again. Her sister was gone. She had no one. Nothing. No, that wasn't true. She had her health, a new business to keep her busy and a town to win over. She was going to change lives, make a difference. It was enough. It had to be enough. She needed to focus.

She opened her eyes, took a deep, steadying breath, stood tall, and stepped out of Patrick's arms. "I'm all right." She gripped the back of a chair at her kitchen table. Wrapping herself in resolve, she turned to look at Patrick. "I've chosen to be alone."

He nodded. "I know. I can see that. But it won't work. We're not wired that way."

"Allowing yourself to be close to someone has nothing to do with how we're wired. It's a choice."

"What about love?"

"That's a choice, too."

His laugh was harsh. "How I wish that was true." He crossed his arms, looking around the room until finally settling his

148

gaze on hers. "No one knows better than me that you can't force yourself to feel something you don't, no matter how much you want to."

Patrick took one long stride, and she was in his arms with him kissing her like she'd never been kissed before, feeling more than she'd ever felt in her life. All those euphemisms were true. She was drowning in sensation, falling hard and fast, hoping that these feelings would never end.

When he abruptly ended the kiss and released her, she had to grab the chair again to remain upright.

"Is what you're feeling now a choice, Frannie?" he said softly. He clenched his hand into a fist and said, "What I'm feeling is raw and powerful and real, and I feel it whether I'm touching you or kissing you, looking at you or thinking about you. The only real choice is if you will acknowledge it or not." He walked to her back door, and with his hand on the knob, turned to face her. "Refusing to accept my own core truths is what made me sick all those years. I won't live like that now. I can't. The way I see it, we've both been given a second chance." He opened the door. "I'm here, Frannie. I'm here." The door closed behind him.

She let him go. When she'd moved to

149

Angel Ridge, she'd decided she would no longer live in fear. But here she stood, alone in her kitchen, still letting fear rule her. She pulled out a chair and sat, wondering what it would take to move beyond that fear and take a chance.

CHAPTER 8

The next day dawned after a sleepless night for Frannie. She wanted to stay in bed. However, knowing that would lead to a day of inactivity she couldn't afford with the Town Hall Meeting only a day away, she got up and took a jog. The troubling fatigue soon had her returning home to shower and dress for work. At the office, she called to see if her medical test results had come back, but ended up leaving a message. Two hours later, she sat at her desk staring at the wall, still replaying her encounter with Patrick in her kitchen.

"Frannie?" Verdi came into Frannie's office, thankfully interrupting her thoughts. "The handouts for the Town Hall Meeting are ready, so I'm going to the printer to pick them up. Do you need anything while I'm out?"

"No, thanks. You know, I think I'll walk over to the diner to get some coffee."

"You look tired, dear. Worrying about the meeting won't do you any good. Besides, everything is going to go well. I'm sure of it."

"Thanks for the vote of confidence, Verdi."

"Anytime. I'll be back soon."

After Verdi left, Frannie grabbed her purse and stood. Making sure she had her keys, she walked downstairs and into the construction zone that would be the retail shop. All work stopped.

"We've got to get you a hard hat," Blake Ferguson said as she picked her way through the space.

"I'm sorry to be such a bother. You have to stop working every time I walk through."

"No worries." Blake held the door and stepped out onto the sidewalk with her. "We should be finished by the end of the week. We're about ready to begin painting."

"That's great," Frannie said. They could be up and running in a matter of weeks, and Blake could begin Phase II of the remodel if they got approvals for the B&B.

"Uh-oh," Blake said.

The smile on Frannie's face froze. Seeing the concern on Blake's face, she knew something was wrong. "What?"

He nodded in the direction he was looking. "Looks like Mrs. McKay is headed this way."

Frannie saw the older woman walking purposefully across the Town Square toward them. "Oh, good. I've been trying to see her, but she's been too busy to meet with me."

"That's one of her strategies for controlling things. Everything on *her* terms."

That was the only warning she had before the woman was upon them. "Ms. Thompson, a moment?"

"Mrs. McKay," Blake said, "a good morning to you."

The older woman gave Blake a sharp look. "In private," she stated succinctly.

"Nice to see you, too." Blake smiled. "Frannie." He nodded, then retreated back into the building.

"Mrs. McKay, it's a pleasure to finally meet you."

"Indeed." She focused on the construction going on in the building behind Frannie. "I see things are moving right along, despite the fact there has been no approval for your scheme by the Town Council."

Smile in place, Frannie said, "I have a business license for a retail shop here. Everything is in order. The Town Council doesn't have jurisdiction over approving businesses opening in town."

"It's a courtesy most extend, not that you would know that since you are an outsider."

"It's my intent to be a good neighbor, Mrs. McKay. All of the Foundation's plans, which you already have in hand, will be outlined in tomorrow's Town Hall Meeting. I very much want the support of the community for this project."

"Forcing this on everyone when there are so many unanswered questions is not the way to proceed," Mrs. McKay said.

"I'm happy to sit down with you to answer any questions you may have. I've been trying to make an appointment with your assistant for some weeks now."

"I am a busy woman with many obligations, Ms. Thompson."

"Of course." Frannie pulled a card from her purse and held it out to Mrs. McKay. "Have your assistant contact mine to schedule a meeting at your convenience."

"That won't be necessary. I will not support this endeavor."

"Excuse me?"

"First your sister comes into town, stirring up all manner of trouble that resulted in bodily harm to some of our residents. Property was defaced, and an explosion disrupted life in our quiet, peaceful town and tragically ended your sister's life, God rest her soul. And now, here you are with a plan to invite a base element into our midst under the guise of 'job training,' " she used her fingers to make quotation marks before continuing, "and even have them *live* here."

Frannie opened her mouth to speak, but was cut off when Mrs. McKay held up a bony hand to stop her.

"No, thank you. Take your charitable enterprise to Maryville or Vonore or some depressed little town further south. We do not want this here in Angel Ridge."

With that, she spun on her serviceable heels and marched back across the Square toward her bank.

"Welcome to the club." Candi Heart approached, smiling. "It's an exclusive group, businesswomen in town that Mrs. McKay hates. She still makes a point to come over to my shop at least once a month to look down her nose at me and everything I sell."

"Really?"

Candi nodded. "She finds me and my shop *tacky* and *base,*" she said, affecting Mrs. McKay's high-pitched, nasal voice while elevating her chin, screwing up her mouth, and looking down her nose. "I could go on."

Frannie couldn't help laughing. It felt

155

good to commiserate with someone who understood being an outsider in Angel Ridge. "It's good to see you, Candi."

"I'm glad to see you, too. I was just about to open when I saw you over here, exchanging words with Mrs. McKay, and I thought I'd come help run interference."

"I appreciate that."

"Power in numbers. Let me fix you a cup of tea," Candi offered. "If you don't mind me saying, you look like you could use it."

The concealer on the dark circles under her eyes clearly wasn't working. "I'd like that." She'd enjoy the conversation as well.

"Ladies, good morning."

"Good morning to you, Mayor," Candi said. "I see you're making your morning deliveries."

Patrick joined them on the sidewalk, all smiles, looking more handsome than he had a right to in khaki slacks and a pale blue polo. He was carrying a box filled with groceries. His smile was rueful. Everything about him drew Frannie in and had her remembering his kiss and the way his arms had felt around her.

"It is Wednesday." He lifted the box in confirmation.

"Am I missing something?" Frannie asked.

"The mayor has been delivering Miss Estelee's groceries to her since he was a kid," Candi supplied.

"And she still expects me to, despite the fact that I haven't delivered for Wallace Grocery since I was a teenager."

"What you're doing means a lot to her," Candi said. "There's something comforting in knowing there are routines and people you can depend on."

"Yeah, well don't spread that around," Patrick said. "It'll ruin my reputation as a hard-edged politician."

"Right," Candi said, laughing, as if the notion of his being "hard-edged" was quite funny. "Well, we won't keep you. Frannie and I were just about to share a cup of tea and some good conversation."

Patrick nodded, walking toward River Road. "You ladies have a nice day."

"You, too, Patrick." Candi looped her arm with Frannie's, and the two walked a few doors down to Heart's Desire. "That was interesting."

"What?" Frannie asked.

"So, you and the mayor, *huh*?" Candi said with a smile.

"What?" Frannie choked out. She cleared her throat and looked around to make sure no one overheard their conversation. "I don't know what you're talking about," she

157

managed with more calm than she felt.

Candi pulled out her keys and unlocked the front door to her shop. "I'm sorry. I sometimes speak out of turn."

Frannie would have responded, but she was distracted by Candi's window display. The sign read, "Naughty and Nice." On one side, there was a pastel nightshirt with a bunny rabbit holding flowers on the front, fuzzy slippers, and an Easter basket filled with colorful plastic eggs. On the other side, there was a pale, lavender teddy that was more lace than substance, beautiful crystal champagne glasses filled with pearls, and high heeled feather slippers that would give a man ideas. Hell, they were giving her ideas.

"See anything you'd like to try on?" Candi asked. "The teddy would look fantastic on you. Lavender is the perfect color to bring out the reds in your dark hair." Candi touched Frannie's hair and said, "A henna rinse would look great in it as well. Why don't you let me give you a trim? I have an organic conditioning treatment you're going to love."

"You do hair?"

"I didn't when I first opened the shop, but there were some ladies in town who wore me down. You see, this used to be the

158

town beauty parlor, and the women were tired of having to go to Maryville to get their hair done. So, I got licensed and put the shop in the back corner of my tea room." She shrugged. "It works. Ladies can chat and have tea while they wait for their appointment."

Frannie looked around. Candi sold clothing and chocolate, did flower arrangements, ran a tearoom *and* a salon? "How do you do it all?"

"I like staying busy. Plus, I schedule most of the salon appointments in the morning when the retail is slower. In the afternoons, I have a lady come in who helps out until closing. Come to the back, and I'll put water on for the tea."

They walked down a long hallway. To one side, there was a "Nice" room, and across the hall, the "Naughty" room. Frannie smiled, imagining what Mrs. McKay would say about whatever Candi sold in the naughty room.

At the back of the building, there was a long spacious room with high ceilings. As Candi had said, to one side, there were small, round tables and a counter. On the other side of the room, a portable screen provided privacy for the salon customers. Candi flipped on lights, then walked behind the counter to run water into an electric kettle and plug it in.

"What I said earlier was that sometimes I speak out of turn, but what I really meant to say was that sometimes I say things people aren't ready to hear." She set two cups on the counter. "I apologize. I need to be more sensitive to a person's receptiveness."

Frannie frowned. "I don't understand."

Candi set out a canister of tea. "I know, but you'll become accustomed to it as you get to know me better. What do you think of this tea?" She held out the canister, and Frannie inhaled the amazing aroma. Cinnamon, citrus, and peach.

"Smells wonderful."

"I just mixed it up last week. Mind being my guinea pig?"

"Not at all. You make tea, too?"

"Yep. Everything in the shop is organic and natural. I make all the skin care products and perfumes, too."

Frannie just shook her head. "How did you learn to do all this?"

"Where I come from, we couldn't go to the store every time we needed something. We made our own." After pouring hot water into a teapot and hanging a stainless steel ball filled with tea in the water, Candi put everything on a tray and carried it to a table. "Sit," she invited. The aroma of the steeping tea filled the air.

"I can't wait to taste that," Frannie said.

Candi filled a cup and handed it to Frannie. "I hope it tastes as good as it smells. Add a little cream and honey."

Frannie fixed her tea, blew on the steaming liquid, then took a sip. "*Mmm . . .* it's fabulous."

"Excellent. This was one of my Aunt Ruby's favorite base teas. You can add any number of fruits and spices to flavor."

"Aunt Ruby?"

"My grandmother. Everyone called her Aunt Ruby, including me. She raised me."

"Up on Laurel Mountain, right?" Frannie supplied.

"Yes. Did I tell you that?"

"My sister mentioned it."

Smiling, Candi said, "Funny, when I think of Jenny, I see her smiling with a baby and a dark, handsome man."

Frannie choked, coughing and sputtering tea into her hand.

Candi passed her a napkin. "There I go again. Speaking out of turn."

"How do you do that?"

"Like I told you, I just know things — always have. Sometimes it feels like a gift.

161

Other times, it seems more like a curse. But mostly, I try to just accept it because it's part of me, a gift from the long line of strong women who came before me."

"How does it work, if you don't mind me asking?"

"Oh, no. I don't mind. It's really a perception. I pay close attention to a lot of things. I trust my senses and my intuition. I see signs in nature that speak to me." She sipped. "I know, it sounds strange, but that's how I was raised. It's the only way I know how to function in the world."

"It sounds like a more natural way to be in the world. Sometimes I think all our conveniences have just made life more complicated."

"And a lot of the things we do work against nature rather than with it."

"I couldn't agree more."

Candi reached across the table and took Frannie's hand. "I know to anyone looking at our situation, it would seem impossible that we could be sitting at a table having a conversation."

Frannie covered Candi's hand with hers. "What happened with Jenny wasn't your fault, Candi. Jenny lived her life on the edge. Something bad was bound to happen sooner or later. She tempted fate too many times."

"I'm just glad you found your way to us," Candi said.

After sharing a moment of quietly absorbing the easy feeling of companionship that existed between them, the two women's friendship settled around them like a comforting blanket. In that moment, Frannie didn't feel quite so alone in the world.

"Can I tell you something?" Candi asked.

"Is this going to be one of those things I may not be ready to hear?"

Candi just shrugged.

Frannie set her cup down. "Go ahead."

"I get the impression that there are strong feelings between you and the mayor, but there's a darkness around you both. Yours seems heavier."

Frannie didn't know what to say to that, so she just waited.

"You've given me your trust, haven't you?" Candi said.

That got to the heart of the matter. "That's different."

"How? Because I'm a friend, I can't let you down?"

"No, you could, but I don't believe you will," Frannie said.

"All of us have the potential to hurt those

we care about." Candi's gentle words seemed to float and land softly in the room without disturbing the mood of safety and acceptance Frannie felt. "Wouldn't you agree?"

"I suppose so. Still, a person's actions say a lot about them."

"True. But be careful not to form opinions about folks based on their past. People grow and change. I know I'm not the same person who settled in this town six years ago. Are you the same person you were six years ago?"

"No, but . . ."

"But?" Candi prompted when Frannie didn't finish.

"I don't know."

"If you and I can be friends despite our past, maybe there's a chance that you and the mayor might be able to find your way to the people you have both become, scars and all."

"I don't know, Candi."

"No. But you will," Candi promised, smiling as she lifted her antique teacup to her lips.

"Well, I was wondering when you would bring my groceries by," Miss Estelee said. "I'm all out of tea, flour and sugar. And you know what happens if I don't get my afternoon sweet tea and sugar cookies."

"We certainly can't have that," Patrick chuckled.

"Bring 'em on into the kitchen. Be sure and wipe your shoes. I just mopped."

"Yes, ma'am."

"I used the last of the flour to make biscuits this morning, and I've got honey. Sit, and I'll pour you a cup of coffee."

Patrick would have told her he had to get back to the office, but it wouldn't have done any good. So, he sat at the table and said, "Thank you, Miss Estelee. You've sure been busy this morning."

The little white-haired lady cackled. "You know what they say. A rolling stone gathers no moss. If I stopped moving, these old bones would surely lock up on me."

"No worry about that happening to you anytime soon."

"Here you are." Miss Estelee set a plate of biscuits and crocks of butter and honey in front of him, quickly followed by a cup of strong, black coffee. Just what he needed after a restless night.

"I'm glad you're here, Patrick. I have a word for you."

In Miss Estelee code, that meant she had gotten a divine message that she intended to share with him. Call it what you would, Miss Estelee simply knew things the average human shouldn't be able to discern. In a different setting, some might call her a fortuneteller, but there was no trick to it. She'd done it too many times for anyone who knew her to question it. She was clearly connected to a higher power, maybe the angels she told everyone she talked to. At any rate, he knew to just listen, accept and deal with what she would reveal.

"Nice. I could use a good word about now."

"Well, it all depends on you if it's to be considered good or not." She sat and faced him across the table.

"I'm listening." He lifted his coffee to his lips and sipped the caffeinated fortification.

"It's time the truth came to light."

He waited, but she said nothing more — just sat there, looking at him like she'd had her say.

"The truth?"

"Yes. All of it. You've been hiding from it for most of your adult life, and it's give you nothing but problems. Now we saw what secrets could do when Ruby's granddaughter, Lark, come to town. Hiding things causes troubles, and that sweet girl that just came to us don't need us to add to hers.

She's the delicate type that don't handle it well."

Shaking his head, he tried to decipher all the messages in that packed statement. "That sweet girl who just came to town? Do you mean Frannie Thompson?"

The older lady slapped the table and pointed a finger at him. "That's the one."

"And you mean the trouble that followed Candi to town because of all the secrets surrounding her mother."

She nodded. "Right again."

"You think my so-called secrets can cause that kind of trouble?" He remembered the explosion that killed Jenny Thompson. He supposed that was the trouble Miss Estelee was saying Frannie had to deal with. But the bit about her being delicate and unable to handle it, he had to laugh.

"What's funny?" Miss Estelee asked.

"You saying that Frannie is delicate. That has not been my impression of the lady."

"She hides it most of the time. Like you, she has two faces. One she shows the world, and another no one sees but her."

"Okay." It was certainly true that for many years he'd had two sides: the upstanding member of the community and the man who drank. Did she mean he needed to reveal to everyone that he was an alcoholic?

"I can see you're unsure," she said.

"A bit," he agreed, "about the secrets part."

"A person with something to hide is a person not to be trusted. Secrets, and the lies involved with keeping them, are no basis for any kind of relationship."

He racked his brain. He had already told Frannie about his drinking. What else could there be?

"The truths you're hiding will cause you more trouble than you can imagine. Better to lay it all bare now."

She stood and cleared the table. "The quilting circle is meetin' down at the church this morning. I need to change and get movin' that way."

Patrick stood. "Thank you for the coffee."

They walked to the kitchen door. After Miss Estelee had opened it, she said, "Think about what I've said, Patrick."

Puzzle over what she'd said would be a more accurate statement. "I will," he said honestly.

Nodding, Miss Estelee said, "See you next week," then closed the door.

As Patrick walked around the house and down to the sidewalk to head back into town, he thought about Miss Estelee's warning and pulled up short. One major

168

secret he'd kept most of his life bloomed in his mind.

He looked at the lake that stretched out below River Road. As he stood on the ridge for which the town was named, staring at the mountains that rose in the distance, he wondered why now. He'd gone through this when he'd stopped drinking and started the hard work to get his life back on track. Keeping the secret went against dealing honestly with people, but since keeping this secret had been Susan's fervent wish, he'd gone along, although doing so had eaten away at him. Why now, when he was finally sober and ready to move on with his life? He'd had two reminders in two days of the one secret he'd vowed never to reveal.

The protocol would be to talk it out with someone. Patrick got his feet moving toward town and pulled out his cell phone to call Pastor Reynolds.

Frannie found comfort and a tension release in the steady rhythm of her feet hitting the pavement as she ran. After completing final preparations for the presentation and going over it again for the umpteenth time, she decided to go home, pull on a T-shirt and shorts, and lace up her shoes. It was a beautiful day, warm with temperatures in the eighties, and she'd felt energized after having tea with Candi. If she timed it right, she could catch the sun setting behind the mountains just beyond the lake. But first, she wanted to go up to what the locals called the Tall Pines above town.

The steep incline from town up to the Tall Pines had her breathing hard and struggling. She hoped the climb to the top would be worth it. She'd heard this was the most peaceful spot in the area, that there was something spiritual about the quiet, open green space.

When she got to the top of the trail, she was not disappointed. The path she'd taken ended at an oval clearing surrounded by pencil pines so tall they appeared to reach up to the heavens. Quiet blanketed the place in a heavy hush that welcomed her in such a way that her labored breathing evened out so the stillness wouldn't be disturbed.

Frannie stood there wanting to soak it all in — the deep blue of the sky just before the sun dipped and the moon took its place, the lush green carpet of grass beneath her feet and the scent of pine laced with the promise of honeysuckle about to bloom. This was one of the reasons she'd left her life in the city. There were so many places near Angel Ridge where she could forget all her troubles and simply marvel at creation.

Frannie closed her eyes, tipped her head back, and inhaled the peacefulness.

Without knowing how much time had passed, she became aware of movement to her right. Movement punctuated by a bird high above taking flight and calling out its fearful protest at having its peace disturbed. She opened her eyes and saw a young girl. It was the waitress from the diner — Patrick's daughter, Abby.

"Sorry. I didn't mean to startle you," Abby said.

"I didn't see you over there."

The girl shrugged, shoving her hands into the back pockets of her jeans. "I like to come up here after the dinner rush."

Frannie took a step toward the girl. A little shorter than Frannie's five foot six height, the top of the girl's head came to about Frannie's nose. Patrick was tall, but not overly so, making her wonder if his wife had been petite like his daughter.

"I'm Frannie. Frannie Thompson."

The girl nodded. "I remember. You had dinner with my dad at the diner the other night." Her gaze locked on Frannie in a manner that made her feel like she didn't quite know if she would trust or accept her.

"It's nice to see you again," Frannie said,

encouraged that the girl hadn't bolted. Something about her spoke to Frannie. She'd pulled her long hair into a ponytail. The dark bangs framing her dark eyes made them stand out prominently. She dyed her hair stark, inky black, a color that she'd replicated on her fingernails and drawn around her eyes. She had incredibly long lashes.

"Is this your first time up to the Tall Pines?" Abby asked.

"Yes. Candi told me about it, so I thought I'd put it on my route."

"You run a lot." It was a statement, not a question. "I noticed since I live next door."

"Ah, yes. It's a good stress reliever for me."

The girl nodded. "I liked your sister," Abby said, surprising her.

"I understand she liked you as well."

Abby nudged a pinecone with the toe of her high top tennis shoe — also black, to go with the rest of her clothes. "I like to write. We had that in common."

"Really?"

"Yeah. She came to the middle and high school and worked with girls after school, encouraging us to write. She told us about jobs and stuff good writers could do."

Frannie took another step in the girl's

direction. "I'm sure she enjoyed that very much."

"She gave me a journal when my mom got sick. Said it helped sometimes to write down what you're feeling, especially if you're like me with no one to talk to."

"You had your dad."

Abby kicked the pinecone into the clearing, forcing Frannie to take a step back or be hit. "He was never around much. I couldn't talk to anyone the way I did my mom."

Absorbing that disturbing bit of information about Patrick reminded Frannie of her own dysfunctional family. "I had that kind of relationship with my sister," Frannie found herself confiding. "I miss having her to talk to."

Abby nodded, still looking at Frannie with that unblinking gaze that seemed to take in everything at once. "I should get back. Dixie and I have to roll the silverware for tomorrow."

Like any good writer, she had a proper grasp of diction for a girl her age. Jenny would have appreciated that. The girl turned to go, and Frannie found herself saying, "Feel free to come over to my house, Abby. Anytime. I'd enjoy the company."

Abby stopped and looked back at Frannie

over her shoulder. Her face held that same expressionless look, but her eyes spoke volumes. The girl was sad and so lonely. Frannie knew the feeling, and she had the irrational urge to go to Abby and put her arms around her the way Patrick had done for Frannie last night. But that was a gesture she, a stranger to the girl, couldn't offer. So she waited, hoping Abby would at least find sincerity in her invitation.

At length, Abby said, "Okay," and then she turned and hurried down the hill toward town.

Frannie let out her breath, and looking around the clearing felt a lightness in her chest that hadn't been there since she'd arrived in Angel Ridge. Maybe Candi was right. Maybe there was something magical about this place. Given the connection she'd made with Candi, and now possibly Abby and Sammy, maybe some of that magic had seeped into her own life without her noticing. It didn't escape her notice that she'd connected with the mayor's children. Could that be a sign that she could trust her heart with him?

CHAPTER 9

Patrick came home early to help Sammy cut Frannie's grass. It was an unusually warm, early spring day, humid and in the eighties. They made a good team with Sammy on the push mower and him manning the weed eater. After they'd finished, he went back home, fixed sandwiches for the two of them, and then showered. Sammy packed a change of clothes in his backpack and headed over to the diner. Both of his kids usually spent the night with Dixie on Wednesday nights, their midweek break from Patrick, as Dixie called it.

After seeing Sammy off, Patrick went back over to Frannie's to pull the mower out of her utility building and work on getting it to run. He'd picked up the supplies he needed earlier from the hardware store and set about replacing the fuel line, the oil and filter, spark plug, and then he was going to take the blade off to sharpen it.

He didn't know how long he'd been at it when he heard the gate on the privacy fence squeak, and Frannie ran into the backyard. Without breaking stride, she went right over to the water hose, stripped out of her damp T-shirt, kicked off her sneakers, and turning on the water, doused herself. Patrick stood, wiping his hands on a rag, and drank in the sight of her in only a sports bra and a brief pair of shorts, water sluicing down her body.

He'd been concealed from her view at the side of her wooden utility building. He should make his presence known, but he couldn't tear his eyes away from the sight she presented. Desire, hot and hungry, rocked him.

He must have made a sound, because she turned toward him, startled from the enjoyment of her impromptu shower. She dropped the hose, and it bounced on the patio, spraying water in all directions until she bent to shut the water off.

Grabbing her drenched T-shirt, she held it in front of her. "Patrick! What are you doing here?"

He took a step in her direction, and then another and another. Tipping his head toward the mower, he said, "I thought I'd try and get this going. I'm sorry, but I didn't have time to warn you that I was here before, *um,* you . . ." He motioned toward the hose but couldn't take his eyes off her, standing there dripping wet, looking hotter than any teenage, pinup fantasy. Words failed him, and any politician worth his salt was never at a loss for words, but Frannie did things to him no woman ever had.

"The mower?" Her blue eyes darkened as he stared at her. She blinked slowly, goose bumps erupting across her arms and long, long legs.

Patrick smiled and stepped closer. She felt it, too.

"Yes, the mower," he said softly. He lifted a thick strand of dark, damp hair off her cheek and tucked it behind her ear. "I know you said you'd have someone look at it, but I wanted to fix it for you."

"Why?" she said hoarsely.

The grease on his hands had made a black streak on her wet cheek that now ran down to her jaw. "Sorry," he said, but he had no way of getting it off.

"What?"

He grasped the edge of the T-shirt she had clutched against her chest and wiped her cheek, but then he got grease on her T-shirt. Her gaze shot down to his chest and then lower. She wet her lips, and then took her time bringing her velvety blue eyes back to his.

"I need to wash my hands," he said. "Can I come into your kitchen?"

She nodded, but didn't speak. Her lips were slightly parted, and he could see her heartbeat throbbing at the side of her neck. God, he wanted her, and seeing the physical evidence that she wanted him, too, added fuel to the fire.

He clenched his fists and walked around her, entering her house through the kitchen door just off the patio at the back of her house. He turned on the water at the sink, then poured a generous amount of dish-washing soap onto his palms and scrubbed the grease from his hands. Frannie followed. He glanced her way. She'd put her wet T-shirt back on, but the way it clung to her body was hotter than when she'd been without it. He had to get out of here, or he couldn't be held responsible for his actions.

The door clicked softly closed. She didn't turn on the light despite the fading sun weakly coming through the window in front of him. Taking her time, she approached him. She stopped close, too close, leaning a hip against the counter as she watched him. He could see in his peripheral vision that she'd wrapped one arm around her waist

178

and propped her other arm on it while she chewed on the side of a finger, making him wonder what it would be like if she used her teeth on him.

And that did it. He rinsed his hands, and without drying them or shutting the water off, reached out an arm and pulled her hard up against him from shoulder to hip. When he took her lips, the kiss was hard, hot and needy. Screw gentle and making sure she was ready for it. He slanted his mouth against hers, wet and open, angling her head with a hand at the back of her head so he could go as deep as he wanted. She responded completely, meeting every thrust of his tongue with one of her own.

She reached over and turned off the water, but didn't break the kiss. A moan that started deep in his throat rumbled in his chest as he fitted his hands to the curve of her bottom, then lower to her thighs. He lifted her up onto the counter and pulled her shirt up over her head. She got to work on freeing her hair from its restraint until it spilled, damp and curling over her shoulders and down her back.

Breaking the kiss then, he let his mouth move down to her neck where he tasted a sexy, earthy combination of salt and spigot water. When she wrapped her legs around his waist and pulled him closer with her ankles against his thighs, he nearly came unglued. He tugged at the straps on her shoulders, but the design of the sports bra frustrated them both, so he settled for resting his hands at her sides, his thumbs teasing the wide elastic band below her breasts.

An unwanted thought in the back of his mind warned he should disentangle himself and take a step back, but the thought of it seemed completely absurd. He wanted Frannie — it felt like he'd wanted her forever, but . . .

She thrust her fingers into his hair, pulling his lips back up for her kiss. She looked wild and sexy and so achingly beautiful, it made him weak. All he wanted to do was carry her into the bedroom where neither of them would get any sleep tonight.

"Patrick." She moaned his name in a throaty way that went straight to his gut.

It would be so easy to strip off her bra and shorts, unzip his pants and take her here on the counter with her legs wrapped around him, and up against the wall, in the shower, then on the bed, all night long.

She pulled his T-shirt over his head and explored every inch of exposed skin as she went, until all the nerve endings in his body screamed for the release it knew was so close, but . . .

Even with her lips on his neck and her nails digging into his back before trailing down lower to the waistband of his jeans, he knew it would only be sex. Amazing, unbelievable, incomparable sex that wouldn't even come close to quenching his desire for Frannie. And that was the problem. He wanted more than just sex with her. So much more.

But to have more, she first had to know she could depend on him so that then, she might begin to trust him. Maybe, even love him.

And that was it. He wanted more than the bone jarring satisfaction they would experience now. He'd waited his whole life to feel this way, and he wanted it all. He wanted the closeness that came from sharing not only his body with someone, but also his soul, his strengths and weaknesses, and the knowing that no matter the disappointments life brought, they'd share all of it together.

He guided her lips back to his. This time, his kiss was slow, deliberate, soothing, the kind he hoped told her how much he cared for her.

He broke the kiss, trailing the backs of his fingers along her cheek, memorizing the smoky look of desire in her eyes. Heady desire for him.

"What's wrong?" she asked.

"Nothing."

She frowned. "I don't understand."

He put an arm around her shoulders, then stepped to the side and, with an arm beneath her knees, lifted and cradled her against his chest. Frannie smiled and pressed her lips to his temple. Dear Lord, a lifetime of loving this woman wouldn't be nearly enough.

He carried her into the living room and sat on the couch with her cradled against his chest, her thighs across his, her feet pressed against his calf. She leaned in to kiss him, but he turned his head slightly and kissed the corner of her mouth instead.

She frowned. "What's wrong?" she asked again.

Brushing her hair back from her cheek, he just looked at her, memorizing every feature.

"You don't want me?"

He laughed. "I want you," he said, his voice hoarse, rough.

"Then why? I don't understand."

"I need you to know how I want you, too."

She smoothed her hand over his hair. "Tell me."

"First, I'd like for you to tell me some things." She stiffened and eased back away from him, but he caught her with an arm behind her shoulders, not letting her retreat. "You've treated me with distrust and held me at a distance. You've been angry with me, and I understand. But now, you're willing to forget all that and make love with me?"

Frannie turned her head.

"Why do you want me now, Frannie? Even though I want it more than anything, I don't think you could have changed your mind about me. I haven't had the opportunity to show you the man I'm trying to be now."

She chewed her lower lip, then looked back at him. "It's no secret that there's attraction between us."

"And you thought maybe if we acted on it, that it might go away?"

Back to not looking at him, she lifted a shoulder. "What about you? You've made no secret about wanting me, and now that I'm willing, you want to talk?"

She tried to slide off his lap, but he hooked an arm around her legs, again not letting her go. "I want more than just sex with you."

A clock ticked somewhere in the room. A single lamp provided the only light.

"That's all I can offer you now," she said.

"So, are you saying you prefer strictly

sexual relationships? No emotional attachments?"

"Yes. I find it hard to believe you, or any man, would have a problem with that," she said, but again, she didn't look at him, saying without words she wasn't being honest. She tried to distract him by trailing a tempting finger down his chest.

Grasping her hand, he brought it to his mouth and pressed a kiss to her palm. "That's because you don't know me . . . yet."

"Even if I was inclined, I don't want a man in my life."

"Why?"

The veil of aloofness he hated fell into place across her features. "My reasons are my own. If that doesn't work for you, leave."

"I'm not going anywhere."

Smiling, she leaned in, pressing her lips to his. "Good."

He pulled back.

"What now?" she said, clearly exasperated.

"There are some things I need you to hear." It was time for him to speak those truths Miss Estelee had reminded him about. Then, maybe Frannie could begin to trust him.

Wrapping her arms around his neck, her body pressed to his, Frannie said, "I don't want to talk."

He put his arms around her and shifted, laying her down on the couch as he leaned over her, stretching her legs out over his hip. "Humor me," he insisted.

"Don't think you can dominate me, Patrick," she warned.

"I wouldn't want to. Just let me say this, okay?"

She crossed her arms. "All right."

He trailed his fingers from her shoulder to her elbow, then across her tense forearm. "I told you that I'm an alcoholic, that if Susan hadn't been sick, I would have found some other reason to drink."

"I remember."

"But there were reasons that I drank. Reasons why I wanted to keep myself numb so I wouldn't have to —"

Frannie pressed her fingers to his lips, stopping his words. "You don't have to tell me. I don't need to know."

He pulled her hand away. "*I* need you to know. I had so many lies in my life, one just led to another, until it all became too much for me. So, I drank to escape."

"What lies could have been so bad that they led you to drink and pull away from your family, and probably, your friends, too?"

"Susan and I married right out of high school." He paused, trying to form the bitter poison on his tongue into truth. "She was pregnant."

Her gaze locked on his, then she smiled, looking away, then back at him. "Okay. So, you got her pregnant and married her. That's the lie?"

He shook his head. "No. That's not the lie. Everybody knew she was pregnant when we married, because Abby came six months later."

"Just say it then, Patrick. Clearly, I'm not good at guessing."

He placed a hand at the side of her face and held her gaze so she would see the truth of his words when he spoke. "Susan, Dixie, Jonathan Temple, Cole Craig, Grady Wallace, Blake Ferguson and I were all best of friends in high school. We were inseparable. Susan and I dated on and off, Grady and Jonathan both wanted to date Dixie. She went out with Grady a few times, but she had it bad for Jonathan. He was a flirt and popular; he had a lot of girls. It was all on again, off again. But the friendship between us was steadfast." He paused, dragging in a deep breath before continuing. "Dixie and Susan were always best friends — like sisters, but they were in love with the same guy. Susan felt like the worst friend for it and never wanted Dixie to know. She confided in me, but no one else."

"So, you're saying Abby wasn't — isn't . . ." she corrected.

"Abby isn't my child biologically," he supplied, "but she is my daughter in every way that matters. I couldn't love her more if she were mine."

Frannie nodded. "You loved Susan, but she loved someone else. Had a child with someone else." Frannie touched his face, sympathy filling her expressive eyes. "How awful for you. And you married her anyway."

"Not quite." He caressed her cheek with his thumb. "I married Susan because she needed a husband and a father for her baby. She never wanted Dixie or Jonathan to know the truth." He paused. "The only thing Susan and I ever had between us was friendship."

"But you were married for years. You had Sammy."

Patrick closed his eyes. "I tried. I tried to love her and be a good husband to her, a good father to our children. But I failed on all counts."

"That's why you drank."

"Yes," he admitted.

A hush fell across the room; the only

187

sound was the clock ticking. After several moments had passed, Frannie looked back at him. "So, Jonathan doesn't know."

"He figured it out later, after Susan and I had married. He wanted to be a father to Abby anyway, but Susan convinced him to honor her wishes about keeping the secret." Patrick kissed her cheek before continuing. "You see, Jonathan and Dixie were supposed to go to senior prom, and I was taking Susan, except Dixie and I got the flu and couldn't go. We insisted Jonathan and Susan go together."

"Were he and Dixie a couple?"

"Yes. In fact, they dated while he was in college, too. But Jonathan felt so guilty about cheating on Dixie, he ended it." Patrick shook his head, remembering how devastated Dixie had been over the break up.

"So, are you saying that you and Susan weren't a couple at the time?"

"No. Just friends."

"Then why did you marry her?"

"Her father always drank heavily and could be abusive. We both feared what he'd do when he found out about the pregnancy."

"Is he still around?"

Patrick shook his head. "The drinking finally took its toll a few years after we married. Her mother tried to repair her relationship with Susan, but Susan couldn't get past her mother not getting them away from all the years of abuse they'd both suffered at her father's hands."

Frannie eased a hand around his neck. "Where is she now, Susan's mom?"

"After Susan's dad died, she moved to Florida to live with a sister. She came back and stayed with us after Susan got sick. Healing their relationship was good for them both, and good for the kids, too, to have their grandmother in their lives. They go visit her a few weeks every summer."

They sat quietly for a few moments, then Frannie surprised Patrick by saying, "It was kind of you to marry her."

"But at the same time, it was wrong."

"You were both very young."

"I don't regret what I did. I couldn't because we had two amazing children together, but . . ."

"You didn't love her," she supplied.

"It's more than that." He had to look away from the understanding in her eyes because he didn't deserve it. "A better man could have handled the situation. I was selfish and weak."

"What makes you think that?"

"Because, as time passed, I wanted more.

189

I wanted real love, real passion, and I hated not being able to make myself feel those things for Susan." He grabbed a fistful of the sofa cushion. "I could never get out of my head that she loved someone else, that she probably longed for him when she kissed me, made love with me." He ground his teeth against the old hurts and deceptions flooding his memory. "The drinking separated me from my family. In the end, I wasn't really there for them."

"Why are you telling me this?"

He grasped her shoulders, squeezing, his eyes locked on hers. "Because I need you to know that my feelings for you are genuine. What I feel for you is strong and intense and deep, but most of all, it's true. For the first time in my life, I feel something that's real . . . for you."

Frannie scrambled off the couch. This time, Patrick let her go. She crossed the room and folded her arms, her back to Patrick. How had this situation turned from what could have been a night of sex she'd likely never forget, to Patrick talking about wanting something more? He might be willing to open up and share his past with her, but there was no way Frannie would do the same.

She heard Patrick approach, and she

turned, but when he would have reached out to take her into his arms, she stepped away from him and began pacing the room.

"Patrick, I get that what you're feeling is real and intense, perhaps even more so because you may have never felt this way before, but that doesn't change anything for me."

"I know. Before you can allow yourself to care about me, you need time to get to know me. How else could you trust that I'm the kind of man you can depend on?"

She folded her arms, shaking her head. "You don't understand. That won't happen. I won't care for you that way. I can't." She'd cheated death once. She wouldn't be so lucky a second time. And even if her health remained good, she definitely couldn't go through losing someone else the way she had lost Jenny. In the end, people always left her. Having friends was one thing, but forming a deeper relationship with Patrick was another thing entirely.

"Why?" he asked.

Frannie had to turn away from the hurt in his pale eyes. "I told you. I don't want a relationship, with you or anyone else."

He nodded. "A strictly sexual relationship, no emotions involved."

"Right." She couldn't give him anything more.

"You don't mean that."

She smiled and laughed a little. "I do," she insisted. No matter how much she might wish for more with Patrick, she wouldn't let herself go there.

Patrick had trailed her around the room until he maneuvered her into a corner, then slowly moved in. When he touched her waist, she flinched, but he slipped his arm around her anyway, pulling her toward him. "Let me care for you, Frannie. Let me be the one you turn to in the middle of the night when you need someone. Let me hold you when you're sad, celebrate with you when you're happy, sit quietly with you and just be."

She shook her head, but longing bloomed in her chest, soft and delicate.

"It's okay to need someone. You don't have to be so strong."

Still shaking her head, she said, "No," her fists clenched against his chest. "I can't."

"Because you've been disappointed before?"

She splayed her hands on his chest, closing her eyes as his words hit too close to the truth. Her tears betrayed her, spilling down her cheeks. Angry, she swiped at them with the back of her hand. "The only person you can count on is yourself. It's really better that way because then, no one can let you down, and you won't let them down either."

"I won't let you down, Frannie."

"You can't make that promise. You don't know what might happen."

Understanding lit his eyes. "You depended on your sister and lost her. Maybe a man has let you down, too, and possibly your parents. I don't know, but I want to." He tenderly brushed away the tears on her cheeks. "Don't you long to have someone you can be close to? Someone you can share your life with?" When Frannie couldn't respond to the truths he'd nailed, he whispered, "Come here," and pulled her into his arms. She resisted at first, but his arms showed her the strength she could find there if she wanted it. "It's okay. I'm here."

"You're here now," she said, turning her face into his neck, her head on his shoulder, body stiff, but wanting to ease into him.

"I'm here now," he agreed. "Because now is all we have." As she shook her head, Patrick cupped the back of her head. "What is it?" he asked against her hair.

"I can't risk it — being close to someone and then losing them," she said, her voice breaking along with her heart. "You of all

193

people should understand how that feels."

His arms tightened around her. "Caring about someone is the ultimate risk. It may be safer to choose isolation. It's good, I suppose, if you're happy that way, but I don't think you are."

After a moment, Frannie pressed her hands against his chest and looked up at him. "What makes you such an expert on me? You don't know anything about me."

"The conflicting emotions in your eyes tell me so much." He pressed his lips to her temple, and Frannie closed her eyes. "I understand the caution," he said. "But that doesn't mean we should just ignore what's going on between us."

"Don't do this, Patrick. Trust me, I'm wrong for you."

"Let me be the judge of that."

Exhausted from fighting what she felt, Frannie slid her arms around his waist and after releasing a sigh, relaxed into him. Nothing had ever felt as right as his arms around her.

After several moments had passed, he said, "Let me fix you something to eat." He smoothed a hand up and down her back.

"What about your kids?" she asked.

"They're at Dixie's tonight."

She could feel all her walls slipping. She

should tell him to leave, but she knew she wouldn't. Not tonight. Tonight, she'd allow herself to need someone. But just for the night.

"I should get out of these wet clothes." She took a step back.

Letting her go left Patrick feeling cold, empty. It should scare him, the power she held over him, but like a siren's call, it only drew him in deeper. "I'll go see what I can put together in the kitchen," he offered.

"I'm not hungry, but . . ."

An excruciating pause lingered in the air. Patrick waited, not speaking, not moving. Her gaze slid from his face to his bare chest, to his waist and lower, then slowly made its way back up.

"Stay?" she said at last.

Nodding, he let out the breath he'd been holding as he watched her walk away. Slow, he cautioned himself. He had to take it slow with Frannie, or she'd bolt. Or worse, they'd wind up making love, ending with her kicking him out of her house and her life.

He turned, retraced his steps to the kitchen, and finding his T-shirt, pulled it on. He heard the shower cut on in another part of the house. The image that came to mind of her naked and wet only a few feet away nearly brought him to his knees. "Slow," he mumbled to himself. Good God, the woman would be the death of him.

He smiled. What a way to go.

Patrick went back to sit on the couch, spending the next few minutes fighting the strong urge to join her in the shower. He needed a distraction, so he focused on the living room where he sat. Maybe he could get some useful clues about her if he paid attention.

It was a beautiful space, tastefully decorated, comfortable with a plush couch, a chaise and an armchair all arranged around a low, antique marble top table. A few boxes sat neatly stacked near a bookcase. The colors were lost on him, along with the pictures hanging on the walls. Instead, he saw himself and Frannie on each piece of furniture, naked and tangled in each other's arms. He eased his hands down his thighs, trying to adjust the fit of his jeans that had been getting tighter since Frannie had her impromptu shower outside. This was pure torture.

"You're still here."

Frannie stood behind the couch, her hair wet and falling loose down her back. She'd pulled on a fitted, soft yellow cotton shirt with a V-neck and dark knit shorts that revealed the enticing length of her long, gorgeous legs. There was something incredibly intimate about being alone with Frannie in her house, the darkness outside lending a feeling of seclusion and privacy. He held out a hand, and she walked toward him, slipping her hand into his, giving him a bit of her trust. He pulled her down next to him on the couch.

"What do we do now?" she asked.

"We don't have to do anything," he said, but felt like his heart would explode when she leaned into him, her head on his shoulder, her hand on his chest.

"You put your shirt back on," she said as she brushed her fingertips across the soft, faded cotton.

He smiled, placing his hand over hers as he wrapped an arm around her. "Is that a hint of disappointment I hear in your voice?"

"*Mmm . . .*" He could feel her smile. "Now that I've seen you without it, it's hard to not think about it." She paused, then added, "Don't let it go to your head."

"That's a tall order," he chuckled.

"There's no question about the attraction between us. If you'd just focus on that and not ask for more . . ."

She slid her hand down his chest and then under the hem of his shirt. The muscles of

197

his stomach clenched against the intense pleasure he felt with her hand on his skin. The problem was his greed. He wanted this and so much more, now and years from now.

"Don't get me wrong," he said slowly, "I'd like nothing more than to take you into the bedroom and spend all night making love to you." To prove his sincerity, he pressed his lips to the pulse beating frantically at the side of her throat. She moaned and leaned into him, inching his T-shirt up with the movement of her hand splayed across his abdomen. His lips skidded up to her ear where he nipped at the lobe, then tugged it into his mouth. While he still had control, he swallowed hard and whispered, "But the morning always comes, and we'd both feel empty and alone when we went our separate ways. You deserve more, Frannie. We both do." He caressed her cheek, tipping her face up until their eyes locked.

"I choose safe relationships with men." She looked beautiful sitting next to him with her legs curled beneath her, no make-up, and her hair not styled. She touched his hand. "You, Patrick Houston, are not safe."

On one level he was flattered, but he knew to Frannie, this was a negative. "You don't know that."

"I know that you have secrets, that we both have secrets that could hurt people if they came to light."

"You mean the secrets about my family?"

"Yes. And what if people close to you found out about that night we shared in the bar?"

Patrick thought about that for a moment, but he knew exactly what he wanted. "It was wrong, but it happened. We can't change it."

Frannie touched her fingertips to his bottom lip. "True," she admitted.

He pulled her close, settling her head against his shoulder once again. "When I got sober, I learned that in order to stop myself from taking that next drink, I needed to ground myself in the present. To not think about what might be or what could have been. I've had to learn to focus on what I have in front of me. Most days, all I can hope for is getting through it without taking a drink."

"Still?" she said.

"Always. Point is, I know I can't change the past or predict the future, but I do my best to make good decisions and live life the best I can, one day at a time. If I do the right things today, like being present for my family and working hard to do a good job

199

as mayor, that makes doing it again tomorrow a little easier." Tracing circles on her arm, he said, "I've had too many regrets that resulted in me wreaking havoc with my life and the lives of those around me. I can't do that anymore." Framing her face with his hands, he said, "We are not a bad decision, Frannie. We can't be. The pull between us is too strong. I have to believe this is happening for a reason."

Closing her eyes, she grabbed handfuls of his shirt, battling the emotions that played across her face.

"We can take it slow," he suggested. Sensing there might be a crack in her wall, he waited.

At length, she said, "Could we start with you just holding me?"

In answer, he stretched out on the couch and pulled her up against his chest. Their legs tangled, and he rested his chin on her head.

Sometime in the night, Patrick woke, and disentangling himself from Frannie, stood and carried her into the bedroom. He laid her on the bed, then pulled up a blanket from the bottom of the bed to cover her. Stretching out beside her, he got under the blanket, too, and folded her back into his arms. They fit together so naturally they were like one person. Having her next to him gave him the peace and deep satisfaction he needed to sleep through the night. He couldn't remember the last time he'd done that.

CHAPTER 10

Frannie woke the next morning, sunshine spilling into her bedroom around the drawn curtains, with birds singing happy songs outside her window. She smiled, stretching. She couldn't remember when she'd slept so soundly. Then she noticed that instead of being under the covers, she was tucked into her nap blanket that usually rested at the end of her bed. That's when it came back to her.

Patrick.

She turned and looked at the pillow beside hers, noting the indention where his head had rested. Sitting up, she pulled the pillow against her. Just inhaling the dark, spicy scent of his cologne set off a longing that made her ache. He'd spent the night, and they'd done nothing but hold each other. With that need for human contact slaked, she'd slept, really slept for the first time since she'd lost her sister. The knowledge that he could affect her so profoundly should have scared her senseless, but instead, she felt refreshed, happy and hopeful.

Bouncing out of bed, she followed the scent of coffee wafting from the kitchen. Was he still here?

On the counter beside the coffee pot, she found a rose from the garden and a note that read:

> I can't tell you how much being with you last night meant to me. Sorry I had to leave so early, but I have a meeting. I'll be at the diner later for breakfast, if you'd like to join me.
>
> Love, Patrick

Frannie held the note to her chest and inhaled the scent of the red rose. She'd enjoyed being with him last night, too, but would meeting him at the diner for breakfast mean taking this to the next level? She couldn't imagine seeing him again after this without everyone knowing that something had shifted between them. He'd said they would take it slow, but in a small town, that might be unrealistic. First steps were often difficult, but she felt willing to test the waters.

Back in her bedroom, she chose a pale

blue maxi dress that had small white flowers embroidered along the high waist and hemline. Several strands of white and blue beads at her neck and wrist, with white hoop earrings completed the summery look. Letting her hair dry on its own last night had brought out the curl, so she brushed it and pulled it back into a high ponytail. A little make-up and some coral lipstick, and she was out the door.

What a beautiful day.

As she walked down Ridge Road toward town, the mountains behind the lake looked gorgeous. A rare clear day allowed the bright sunshine to outline the ridges and valleys of the mountains that were usually obscured by the blue haze that gave the Smoky Mountains their name. The lake stretched out below, blue-green and calm, and she had to stop to take it all in.

"It's a beautiful day to be alive and be livin' on the Ridge, ain't it?"

Frannie turned and saw Miss Estelee leaning against her porch railing, enjoying the view as well. "Yes. Good morning, Miss Estelee."

"Good mornin'. It's a big day for you."

In more ways than the woman could know. "Yes," Frannie said. "I hope you're planning to come to the Town Hall Meeting tonight."

"Oh, yes. I wouldn't miss it. Come closer, and let me have a good look at you."

Frannie smiled and strode up the woman's sidewalk. The gingerbread trim in the eaves of the old house did indeed have angel wings in it.

"Well, ain't you just the picture of spring?" Miss Estelee smiled down at her. "You've got nice color in your cheeks, too. If you don't mind me saying, you was lookin' a mite pale that first time I seen you in Town Square."

"Yes, *um,* I'm feeling well," Frannie sputtered.

Miss Estelee clapped her hands and rocked back on her heels. "I bet you are. Love'll do that to you." The woman's sweet laughter floated on the spring air and swirled around Frannie, leaving her feeling happy and lighthearted rather than shocked at her words. "I told your sister before she left us that she was going to find the man of her dreams and fall in love. I believe you found yours and fell in love about the same time as her. Ain't that somethin'?"

Frannie frowned. Jenny and Cord had found each other years ago, before she'd gone into the Witness Security Program. The same time she'd met Patrick in the bar.

About to utter a denial, Frannie's words were halted when Miss Estelee lifted her hand. "Now, there's no use denying it. It's clear as day to anyone who cares to look close enough. I know the timing was wrong before, but today's a new day."

Smiling, Frannie nodded. "It is indeed." She refused to let her thoughts wander back in time.

Miss Estelee nodded, clearly pleased. "Patrick's a good boy and deserves a new start in life, just like you. His big heart and the way he cares for people sometimes take him down the wrong road, but a heart like that will always find its way home. Yep, better days are ahead."

"I hope so," Frannie said, absorbing the meaning buried in the wise woman's words. Miss Estelee and Candi had a lot in common.

Miss Estelee looked up at the bright sky and declared, "A big storm's a comin', such as this town ain't seen in a long while."

Looking up at the clear sky, Frannie wondered if Miss Estelee was speaking figuratively or literally. On such a beautiful day, Frannie couldn't imagine it. But then, storms always came when you least expected them.

"We'll weather it together," Miss Estelee

continued, "like we always do. Yep, the people of this town might disagree on most everything, but we stand shoulder to shoulder on what's important." Piercing Frannie with a look that wouldn't let her go, she said, "You'd do well to remember that, missy. Real love happens only once or twice in a lifetime. Don't you think to go throwing it away, now. Lean on it and trust that it'll keep you safe when the storms of life come."

After holding Frannie's gaze long enough for her words to sink in, Miss Estelee said, "I'll let you get on to your business. I'll be seeing you tonight."

With that, Miss Estelee turned and walked into her house, leaving Frannie standing in front of her porch, wondering what had just happened.

"Look, the mayor showed up after all," Bud DeFoe said.

"Yes, nice of you to join us," Albert McKay said.

"Sorry I'm late," Patrick said. He looked at his watch. Who in the world, but this group of men, would call six thirty-five in the morning "late"?

Bud handed him a cup of coffee. "Don't pay him no mind," he said, referring to Mr.

McKay. "He just walked in."

"Don't blame me. It's that danged daylight savings time," Mr. McKay complained. "Takes me at least a month to get used to it, and seems like they keep moving it up every year."

All the men in the group mumbled their agreement. They got together most mornings, and even though Patrick couldn't come every day, he tried to come on Thursdays. This was what was affectionately referred to as "the old boys' club." Most were retired or semi-retired, and they liked to gather in the mornings to talk about any and everything. Patrick's dad had encouraged him to join in. He'd learned so much from these wise, older men, and he was thankful to them for that. Something about their steadfast friendships through the years reassured him. There's nothing they wouldn't do for each other.

"Sit, sit," Mr. McKay said. "So, tell us about this Town Hall Meeting tonight. What do you think of that little lady's plan to bring in folks down on their luck, give them job training and help them find jobs?"

"Well, Frannie is the one with all the detailed information about the project," Patrick said. "I'm sure she can answer your questions better than I could. You are planning to come to the meeting, right?"

"Oh, did you hear that, boys? He calls the new gal in town 'Frannie,' " Patrick's Uncle Jim said.

A lot of good-natured laughter lit up the group sitting in the back of the hardware store where Bud had circled up some lawn chairs.

"That's the lady's name," Patrick said. "Since when did we get all formal in Angel Ridge?"

"I saw you talking to her in the park," Bud said.

"And on the sidewalk," his uncle added.

"And they had dinner at the Ferguson's, too," Bud added.

"All right, simmer down, fellas," Patrick said, holding out a hand.

"Sorry I'm late," Grady Wallace said as he walked up to join the group. "What'd I miss?"

"Come on in, Sheriff," Bud said, pouring another cup of coffee. "Patrick here was just telling us about that pretty little lady that's putting the non-profit in my empty buildings on Main Street."

"Ms. Thompson?"

"See?" Uncle Jim said, "His mamma raised him right. Course, *he* ain't got a sweet spot for her."

Another round of laughter overtook the group. So, that's how it was.

"Don't go giving the man a hard time, now, boys," Grady said. "She's a fine lookin' woman, and Patrick here's a single man."

The group fell silent at that comment, uncomfortable at the reference to his wife dying. He did miss Susan, but he felt like a fraud because they all assumed he'd lost the love of his life.

"Not that you noticed, because you're off the market," Bud said to Grady. "Speaking of, when are you and Candi gonna tie the knot?"

"I'm a lucky man, gentlemen. She's putting me out of my misery in June."

"Yours has to have been the longest courtship on record," Patrick teased his cousin.

"You won't catch me complaining," Grady said with a big smile.

"Young people today," Uncle Jim said, shaking his head. "Back in our day, you bought a girl a ring and you married her, then you spent the rest of your life dealing with the impetuous decisions you made when you were too young to know any better."

The older men nodded their agreement, while Patrick and Grady grinned at each other. "That was when men were men, and women were women, right?" Grady said.

"Damn right," Mr. McKay said, "and your parents had more than a little say in who would make a proper wife for a young man. Nowadays, kids could care less what their parents think."

"Martin's still living at home, *huh,* Albert?" Uncle Jim said.

"That boy'll never marry and move out. I'm afraid his mother had too heavy a hand in his raising."

To which everyone just shook their heads. The men in the group had an unspoken understanding that Harriet McKay was difficult and unmanageable, and no one could do anything about it — least of all her husband. None of them thought less of him for it. In fact, they all admired him for putting up with the old battleax all these years. Patrick couldn't imagine.

"So back to your original question, I think *Frannie's,*" Patrick emphasized the familiar use of her first name, let them think what they would, "plan is great. Those buildings on Main have stood empty for too long. What she wants to do will bring new life into the town, and maybe even bring in new residents to buy up some of our goods and fill some of the vacant real estate."

"But what kind of folks do you think she'll

bring into town?" Uncle Jim asked.

Patrick shrugged. "Hard working people who need a break?"

"Who've had a thorough background check," Grady added.

"Those empty buildings make the town look so deserted," Bud said. "I'm glad to have something going in them that'll generate business in town. That's good for all of us."

"I couldn't agree more," Patrick said. Mr. McKay and Uncle Jim looked unsure, so he asked, "Mrs. McKay's already given me her opinion. What do you think, Albert?"

"I think I'll wait until I have all the information before I form an opinion."

"Me, too," Uncle Jim added.

"Glad to see you're all keeping an open mind," Patrick said. Hopefully, after tonight, Frannie would have the support of the town for her business, and with that worry off her mind, she could give more thought to the notion of the two of them becoming a real couple.

About an hour later, when Patrick walked into the diner, he looked around, hoping to find Frannie waiting on him, but she wasn't there.

"Morning, Patrick. Grab a seat anywhere,"

Dixie said.

"Hey, Dixie," he replied, taking a stool at the counter. "Did you and the kids have a good night?"

"Of course. After Abby and I closed up the diner, we settled in at the house and watched a movie until Sam fell asleep. Abby and I stayed up and chatted awhile."

"That's good," he said, glad that Abby had a woman to talk to about girl stuff.

Dixie poured him a cup of coffee. "Can I get you something to eat?"

"No." He glanced over his shoulder as a customer came in.

"Looking for somebody?"

Unable to hold back a smile, he said, "Yeah, maybe."

"Do tell."

The bells on the door rang out again. This time, Patrick turned to see Jonathan Temple slowly making his way to the counter on crutches. "Jonathan." Patrick stood, offering his hand. The two shook, sharing an even look, each taking the other's measure. "I'm glad to see you. I'd like to talk, if you have a minute."

"Sure," Jonathan agreed, taking a seat. "Mornin', Austin," he said to Dixie.

"Jonathan."

Palpable tension flowed between the two,

but that was nothing new. They'd always had strong feelings for each other. They just couldn't seem to keep from hurting one another.

Dixie poured coffee. "You having breakfast?"

Jonathan nodded. "Yeah."

"What'll it be?" Dixie asked, taking out her order pad.

Jonathan's voice dipped. "You know what I like, darlin'."

Patrick choked on his coffee. When he finished sputtering, he said, "Y'all should just get a room and put everybody out of their misery."

"Patrick!" Dixie exclaimed, and she was actually blushing.

"Works for me," Jonathan said nonchalantly, sipping his coffee.

All Dixie could do was point her finger at one and then the other before she disappeared into the kitchen.

"I hope you know what you're doing," Patrick warned.

"What I should have done years ago. You know how I feel about her," Jonathan said.

"Yeah, but you always found a way to break her heart despite that."

"I've made mistakes, but it's time. I want to make things right."

214

"Are you including my daughter in that statement?"

"She's my daughter, too, Pat," Jonathan said softly. "I'd like to get to know her."

"Then get to know her, but as Jonathan Temple, former football phenom who's retiring and moving back to Angel Ridge. Nothing more."

"I've seen her here at the diner. She's beautiful." He paused, then added, "She has my eyes."

"Watch what you say." Patrick looked over his shoulder. "If you hadn't come home to see Dixie that Christmas and done the math, this wouldn't be an issue now."

"I would have married her, done the right thing, but no one gave me the chance."

"That would have killed Dixie. Susan couldn't stand the thought of it. Fact is, Susan made it clear she didn't want Dixie to ever know."

"Secrets like this have a way of festering."

Patrick knew that better than most. "Agreed. Look, if you want to come clean with Dixie, that's between the two of you, but you have to see that telling Abby that you're her biological father would be the wrong thing to do. She's still recovering from losing her mother. She's not ready to have her world turned upside down again."

Nodding, Jonathan poured more cream in his coffee and stirred. "I understand."

"Look, I'm not suggesting that we take this secret to our graves. I'm just saying, not now. I hope you can respect my wishes."

Jonathan turned to Patrick. "You're her father, Pat. That won't change. I just want to be part of her life, too."

That never would have been possible while Susan was alive. But Patrick could see a way clear to bringing the secret into the light at some point. Still, it would kill Dixie.

As if reading his thoughts, Jonathan said, "I can't have an authentic relationship with Dixie until we deal with this."

"Give it some time. No need for y'all to rush into anything."

"I don't remember asking your opinion on the matter," Jonathan said defensively.

"You got it anyway."

The bell on the door tinkled as Frannie entered the diner, but no one noticed. Patrick and Jonathan Temple seemed to be involved in a heavy conversation, so Frannie cautiously approached the two men at the lunch counter. "Good morning," Frannie said. Patrick had asked her to meet him here, but maybe this was a bad time. "Am I interrupting something?"

Patrick stood, his face softening when he

looked at her. "No." He grasped her elbows, smiling as he leaned down to kiss her cheek. Frannie frowned, glancing around to see if anyone observed them. No one seemed to notice except for Jonathan and Dixie, who'd just walked up to the counter from the kitchen. She set a plate of food in front of Jonathan, her eyes wide when she saw Patrick touching Frannie. She took a step back, embarrassed.

Trying to make things less awkward, Patrick said, "Frannie, you remember Jonathan?"

"Yes, of course. How's your knee?"

"A nuisance, but healing."

Jonathan smiled. He was a handsome man with broad shoulders and thickly muscled arms, short dark hair and deep brown eyes. His gaze slid to Dixie, who had trouble meeting his eyes as she busied herself refilling coffee and swiping at the counter with a wet cloth.

"Let me get you some coffee," Dixie said to Frannie.

"Thanks," Frannie said. She saw curiosity rather than wariness in Dixie's eyes as she took in her and Patrick. Frannie held Dixie's gaze, hoping that someday they could be friends.

"Do you have time to join me?" Patrick asked.

Turning back to him, Frannie smiled, remembering how they'd held each other all night. She longed for his arms around her again, but she couldn't help thinking that he might have friends and family who wouldn't welcome her.

"Frannie?" Patrick said.

A movement over his shoulder caught Frannie's eye. She looked, but saw no one — just Dixie and Jonathan watching Patrick and her, openly curious. In answer, she moved toward the counter and sat on the empty stool next to Jonathan. If she got to know his friends better, maybe they'd invite her into their circle, making things easier all around.

Abby stumbled out the back of the diner, tears streaming down her face, her world torn apart. She'd gotten to school and realized she didn't have her backpack. It had surprised the principal when she asked for permission to go to Dixie's and get it. Before, she would have just left school. She did what she wanted. If she felt like laying out or skipping class to sit on the bleachers at the football field, she did. But she'd been trying to do better. Her mom would have wanted that.

When Abby hadn't found her backpack at Dixie's place, she'd come to the diner, remembering she'd left it in the back room next to the kitchen.

Seeing her dad talking to the hunky football player at the counter, she'd been about to walk through the swinging door to say "hello," when she noticed the intense looks on their faces. So, she'd stood there listening. When she heard her name, she'd flattened herself against the wall, then hid behind a shelf just inside the door where she could still hear most of what they said.

They were talking about her, and how the man she'd known as her father her entire life was a complete fraud. He wasn't her father at all. The stranger was. That's when Dixie had breezed through the door, carrying a plate of food and not seeing Abby crouching behind the stacked containers of coffee and tea. Standing, Abby had meant to run to the back door, but she couldn't help taking another look at the man who claimed to be her father. Standing there, she saw more than she'd wanted to when she caught her dad leaning down to kiss their new neighbor on the cheek, smiling at her like some lovesick teenager.

Oh, God. How could this be happening?

Dropping her backpack, she ran blindly through the back alley, away from town.

CHAPTER 11

Frannie could not have possibly been more prepared when the time came for the Town Hall Meeting to begin. She wasn't nervous. Just anxious to win the town's support and move forward with her plans.

Patrick called the meeting to order. He looked handsome in a silvery, gray suit that made his eyes seem almost clear and contrasted with his dark skin and the black wavy hair curling over his starched white collar, which he wore unbuttoned. Shaking her head couldn't dispel the memory of lying in his arms all night long in her bed. Dear Lord, when had Patrick become more than just a distraction?

Verdi nudged her and nodded toward the microphone. Frannie stood, notes in hand, and tugged at the skirt of her coral suit as she made her way to the front of the long room that served as Angel Ridge's courtroom. Filled to capacity, all eyes focused on her. Meanwhile, a sudden spring thunder-storm pounded the metal roof of the old building while wind whistled around the tall windows.

"Thank you, Mayor. I appreciate all of you coming out on such a stormy night. I do promise not to keep you long. Let me begin by explaining what led me to create the Violet Jennings Thompson Foundation."

She then talked about her sister's love of Angel Ridge and how the countless hours she'd devoted to volunteering in the community had given Frannie the beginnings of an idea to do the same. Looking at the areas where the most good could be done, she'd settled on aiding people struggling through the country's economic woes.

"So many people, like Tomas and Lucy Mendez," Frannie indicated the Hispanic couple sitting at the front of the room, "have lost jobs and, as a result of not being able to find other employment, their homes. These are good, hard-working people who are not asking for a handout. They want to work to support themselves and their children, but the jobs just are not available.

"That's where the Thompson Foundation and Angel Ridge can help. By providing temporary housing and job training, we can assist families with securing employment so they can have hope for the future without leaving the area." Frannie paused, looking around the room. "Keeping these good people here provides not only economic stability for them, but also for the town. We keep their jobs, their tax dollars, their mortgages and purchases here, in Angel Ridge. Once the workers have been placed in permanent jobs, the hope is they might then consider purchasing empty houses that have been on the market for some time.

"This is a good thing for both the participants in the program and for Angel Ridge. We appreciate your support as we move forward with this endeavor. Now, I'm sure you have comments and perhaps questions?"

Patrick stood, joining her at the microphone. The warmth of his nearness gave her confidence. "Thank you, Ms. Thompson," he said with a smile just for her. Then turning to the audience, he said, "If you'd please raise your hand to be recognized and then stand to ask your question."

Mrs. McKay raised her hand. Frannie tried to keep her features neutral.

"Mrs. McKay," Patrick said.

The tall, thin woman stood and then waited until everyone's gaze swung her way. "I would like to hear more about what you plan to do with the storefronts you are renovating on Main Street. Also, what businesses in town are, as you say, partnering with you to provide this so-called job training? And how will these *persons* be selected and deemed *appropriate* for your program?"

She looked down her long, straight nose at the Mendez family seated near Frannie. While they certainly were not the face of Angel Ridge, a much-needed dose of diversity would do this town, and particularly its children, a lot of good.

"First, let me say that the people selected for the program must first submit an application, undergo an interview process with myself as well as the potential employer they will be placed with, and additionally, they must agree to a background check that the sheriff conducts.

"The Foundation has partnered with a number of businesses in town to provide diverse types of job training, such as retail with Heart's Desire and DeFoe Hardware, restaurant services with Ferguson's Diner, public service and administrative skills with the Sheriff's Department, the Mayor's Office and the Library, Health Services with Dr. Janice Ferguson, restoration architecture and construction with Ferguson Contractors and CMC Designs.

"As far as the spaces being renovated on Main Street, one structure now houses the Foundation offices. That building will also hold a retail shop on the ground floor where participants and volunteers will operate a thrift shop. The sale of donated items there will help fund job training expenses and housing for the program participants." Frannie smiled as she noticed several people nodding and whispering to one another. "The other two spaces next to this will be converted into temporary housing and a bed and breakfast, which will offer needed housing for the tourists who regularly visit Angel Ridge."

"Well, you simply cannot do that," Mrs. McKay said.

Frannie and Patrick both looked at each other, frowning. "I'm sorry, Mrs. McKay," Patrick said. "Ms. Thompson covered a lot of ground there. What part were you talking about?"

"The bed and breakfast and temporary housing. She can't do that."

"There's nothing —" Patrick began, but was interrupted.

"Town ordinances prohibit use of any of the buildings on Main Street for housing," Mrs. McKay said.

"Permanent housing, yes," Frannie

225

agreed, "but nothing prohibits temporary housing."

"The ordinance prevents persons taking up residence on Main, temporary or otherwise. That area is zoned for retail and commercial use only."

Lightning flashed, closely followed by a clap of thunder that shook the building. Bud DeFoe stood, his hand raised.

"Yes, Bud," Patrick said.

"Pardon me, but that's horse hockey, and you know it, Harriet. Frannie here is right. She and I both checked the town's ordinances before I sold her the buildings. The ordinance you are talking about only keeps people from *living permanently* in the buildings on Main. There's nothing to stop her from going forward with temporary housing." Bud stabbed a finger at Mrs. McKay. "Why, you know as well as I do that a hotel operated for near on to seventy-five years in one of those buildings she plans on using."

"Yes, and you also know as well as I do that establishment closed because of the ne'er do wells who took up residence there, cavorting until all hours of the night, which resulted in robberies and vandalisms, and other things which I hesitate to mention," Mrs. McKay said.

"That was more than fifty years ago, Harriet. No reason to believe that will happen again. Frannie here is working closely with the sheriff, as she said, to screen the people who will be in the program," Bud said before sitting down.

"All right, folks. Let's keep this civil," Patrick warned.

Ignoring that, Harriet continued. "Yes, but why take the chance? I think this is a bad idea all the way around. Let the larger towns in the area with more people and more resources deal with this sort of thing." She waved her hand in the general direction of the Mendez couple sitting at the front of the room, who thankfully, didn't see. "We don't want it in our town." Mrs. McKay took her seat amongst grumblings punctuated with more frequent lightning flashes and thunder outside the tall, glass windows lining the room. The wind was howling around them now, rattling the old wooden frames.

Looking across the unsettled crowd, Frannie saw a thin arm, its hand bent by age, raised.

"Miss Estelee," Patrick said.

The older woman stood with the aid of her cane and Candi Heart's hand at her elbow. "Well, thank you dear," she said sweetly before looking forward and addressing her neighbors. "I reckon I've lived in this town a might near longer than most anyone, and I can tell you, I never seen or heard such as I have these past weeks." Her clear blue gaze swept the room. "Harriet McKay here has spoken, but I've heard more of you say about the same as far as being opposed to this young lady's plan.

"There's no denying, this'll be a big change for our town. It might be uncomfortable for some who are set in their ways." She swung a meaningful gaze at Harriet. "But if you listened closely to the list of businesses in town supporting this, you might have heard that it's mostly the young ones who have stepped up to volunteer their time, talents and resources. Now, we older folks have the years of wisdom and experience, and we are beholdin' to share what we have with folks like these," she gestured with her cane toward the Mendez family and nearly took out three people seated in front of her who ducked just in time.

"Who among us hasn't gone through hard times? Why, this town has suffered fires, floods, depression, recession and bone deep losses of people we love. And we didn't come through it on our own. We come through it by helping and caring for one another. I appreciate that these fine people want to work. I say if we have the means to teach them job skills and give them work for their hands to do, we're bound as Christian folk to do it. The Bible in the book of Hebrews says *"not to forget to entertain strangers, for by doing so some have unwittingly entertained angels."* And a little bit later in that same chapter, it says, to *"not forget to do good and to share, for with such sacrifices God is well pleased."*

"Now, we have been richly blessed here in Angel Ridge. We haven't suffered a lot of the hardships in the past several years some around us have. But we have been guilty of watching our neighbors pack up and leave without us even offering to lend a hand." People shifted uncomfortably in their seats after she spoke that truth. "I don't know about you, but when I take leave of this world, I want it to be said of me that I lived my life in such a way that folks knew they could count on me when they was down and out."

Miss Estelee looked back to Candi, and offering her hand, accepted her help in sitting down. As if to punctuate her words, the heavens let loose a stream of rumbling thunder and bright lighting that captured everyone's attention as it shook the foundations of the building.

Mrs. McKay raised her hand again, and Patrick recognized her about the same time that his son stumbled into the room, drenched from the rain and pale from fright. Patrick caught Dixie's eye and nodded toward the back of the room. Dixie turned, and seeing Sammy, went to him.

Mrs. McKay began speaking. "That's all well and good, Estelee, but everything in order, as the Bible also advocates. If Ms. Thompson wants to use that space in town for residences of any type, it'll have to come before the Town Council for a vote."

Bud DeFoe shot out of his seat. "Well, I'd say we've got a quorum right here. Let's take that vote."

Mr. McKay, the town's legal counsel, stood. "Now, hold on, Bud. Let's don't jump the gun. That's not what this meeting is for. We're here to get information. And besides, we'd need to first examine the ordinance to see if a vote is even warranted."

Harriet McKay gave her husband an icy look, clearly not happy that he'd challenged her assertions regarding one of the town's holy ordinances, of which she clearly considered herself the guardian. Mr. McKay gave her a look right back, providing a bit of indoor fireworks for the town's viewing pleasure.

Patrick stepped up to the microphone, his worried gaze still locked on his son. "Yes, that's right, Mr. McKay. Why don't we take a five-minute break? I believe Ms. Thompson has some refreshments as well as some literature you can look at, if you missed it earlier. Then we'll come back to take any final questions you may have. With the sound of things outside, I think we'd do well to get ourselves home as soon as possible."

Patrick walked quickly to his son as people started milling around and talking to each other. Kneeling before him, Patrick said, "Sammy, what in the world are you doing out in this storm? You're supposed to be home with your sister."

"Abby never come home, Daddy. The power went out, and I was scared with the storm and all. It was so dark."

Patrick folded his son in his arms, knowing how much it cost a boy his age to admit being scared. He smoothed his wet, red curls and said, "It's okay. You're safe now." Looking up at Dixie, he said, "Is Abby working?"

"No. I gave her the night off since everyone in town is here. She knew she was supposed to be home with Sammy. We talked

231

about it last night."

Sammy wiggled out of his arms, but leaned back against Dixie. Oh Lord, what if something had happened to his daughter? He stood, scanning the room to look for the high school's principal. Seeing her, he threaded his way toward her.

"Annalee, can I speak with you?" he asked the middle-aged woman who had taught most of them American History, but had been the middle and high school principal in Angel Ridge for the past ten or so years.

"Of course," she agreed.

"Was Abby okay at school today?"

"I wanted to speak with you about that, Patrick. Abby showed up at school today without her book bag and came to my office to ask permission to go get it. I was frankly encouraged that she asked. As you know, we've had issues with her following rules this year."

"Yes, and I appreciate how patient you've been with her."

"Given the efforts I've seen from her in the past couple of months, I decided to let her go. However, my secretary told me she never signed back in, and her teachers confirmed her absence from their classes."

"She's been gone all day?" Dread was setting in. Abby could be anywhere. Why would she disappear like this? What could have happened?

"Do you mean to say you haven't seen her?" Annalee said anxiously. "I called and left a message at your office. When I didn't hear back from you, I began to worry."

"I was out most of the day," he said, feeling panic rise inside him.

Dixie and Jonathan joined them. "What's going on?"

"Abby left school early today to get her backpack, but never returned."

"Where is she?" Jonathan asked.

"We don't know." Patrick pulled a hand down his face while Annalee wrung her hands.

"Maybe she went to your mom's," Dixie said.

After searching the room and seeing his mother, he caught her eye and motioned her over. When she'd joined them, he asked, "Mom, have you seen Abby today?"

"No, dear. Why?"

Without giving him time to answer, Dixie said, "Patrick, it's storming. If she's out in this —"

He squeezed her shoulder. "I know."

"Abby's out in this?" his mother said, fear making her words high-pitched.

"Folks, let me have your attention." Grady

Wallace had walked to the front of the room to speak into the microphone. "Your attention please." When everyone had settled down, he continued. An eerie hush settled over the room. Even the storm outside quieted. "The National Weather Service has issued a tornado and severe thunderstorm warning. The sheriff in Monroe County just called and confirmed that a tornado has touched down in Vonore, and it's headed this way."

The lights flickered, and then everything went dark. "Stay calm," Grady continued, speaking loudly to be heard. He flicked on his flashlight. His deputy and the constable, who were standing in other parts of the room, did the same. "Please proceed in an orderly manner downstairs to the jail. If you need assistance, wait by the courtroom exit, and we'll make sure you get there safe and sound."

Frannie, somehow, had made her way to Patrick's side, her eyes wide. He reached out and squeezed her hand, pulling her close. Looking back at Dixie, Annalee, and his mother, he said, "I have to go find Abby."

"No one is leaving the building," Grady said, joining them. "The situation outside is extremely treacherous and unsafe."

As if to punctuate his words, the air inside

the room seemed charged, and Patrick's ears popped just before they all heard what sounded like the roar of a train headed right for them.

"Let's go," Grady urged. "Downstairs, everyone. Ladies, children and the elderly first. Men, if you're able, hang back to offer help to those who need it. Dixie, you lead the way. Everyone hold hands. It's dark. Fall in behind Dixie."

"I need to find Geraldine," Patrick's mother said.

"I'll find my mom, Aunt Thelma." Grady said. "You go on ahead."

Dixie nodded. "Right." She clutched Sammy's and Frannie's hands. "Here we go."

Frannie grabbed Mrs. Houston's hand then looked over her shoulder, back at Patrick.

"I'll be there soon," he said, praying that was a promise he'd be able to keep. He went to the doorway of the courtroom, and seeing Miss Estelee, lifted her into his arms. Jonathan stood there, too. Blake and Cole had positioned themselves on either side of him, his arms around their shoulders, as they fell in right behind him. Janice Ferguson stayed close to her husband, Blake, keeping a watchful eye on Jonathan to make sure he was okay. Strangely, no sense of panic invaded the people around him, just one of cooperation with the same urgency propelling everyone forward.

They all made it down the two flights of stairs without incident. Grady and his deputy, Woody, along with Constable Harris did an excellent job directing everyone into the tight space, instructing them to sit on the floor with their backs to the wall, heads between their knees. Patrick remembered all the times he'd done this drill when he'd been a schoolboy, never having to actually use the skill in a real-life situation until now.

He set Miss Estelee on the floor, apologizing that she had to get down on the cold, hard concrete.

"Now, don't you worry none about me." She patted his cheek. "I'm fine. Go on and see to the others."

He turned, searching the faces around him for his son, mother and Frannie. He couldn't help looking for Abby, too, but she wasn't there. Finding Dixie and Frannie helping others line up against the walls, he went to them. The building shimmied, and something that sounded like an explosion rocked them. He tugged Frannie, his mother and his aunt down while Sammy scurried over to him. He somehow managed to put his arms around all of them, shielding everyone with his body, and then he squeezed his eyes shut and prayed.

After what could have been five, or fifty, minutes, he couldn't say which, a stillness settled around them. Everyone looked up in unison, heads swiveling in all directions.

Grady walked through. "Is everyone all right? If you need assistance, Doc Ferguson and Mable are here to help."

"Mom? Aunt Geraldine? Are you both okay?" Patrick asked.

"We're fine, dear," his mother said.

Aunt Geraldine just nodded, her eyes wide and frightened.

When no one spoke up, Grady warned, "Don't get up yet. Woody and I are going out to make sure it's safe. Please be patient."

Frannie had turned her head into the curve of Patrick's neck and wrapped her arms tight around his waist. Sammy pressed into him from the front. Even the unflappable Dixie had tucked herself into Jonathan, who had a worried look on his face.

Over Dixie's head, he mouthed the word utmost on both their minds, "Abby."

Patrick couldn't just sit here knowing his daughter was out there. He nodded at Jonathan and stood, offering him a hand up. "Sammy, stay with your grandma," Patrick said. "We're going to check in with Grady.

Be right back." He made his way to the sheriff, who stood near the rear exit, which was at ground level behind the courthouse. "Grady, Abby is missing."

He nodded. "Clara, you got that?" he said to his dispatcher.

"Yes, Sheriff. I'll add her to the list."

"There's a list?" Patrick said.

"We've evoked the emergency management plan, Patrick. You know the protocol. It's bad up there," he said, referring to the state of the town.

"You've walked upstairs?" Patrick asked.

"There is no upstairs," Grady said. "It's gone."

"Dear God. Are we structurally sound here?"

"Blake and Cole are outside assessing that now."

"We have to get these people out of here," Patrick said quietly, but urgently.

"And we will, as soon as we determine the safest way to do that."

"I need to go look for Abby, Grady."

"I'm going with him," Jonathan said.

"I wouldn't worry. She's probably at home, safe and sound."

"That's assuming we all still have homes," Patrick said.

Grady clapped a hand on Patrick's shoulder. "We'll see our way through this, whatever we find out there."

Patrick nodded. "Sammy said Abby didn't come home, and the school principal said she left school early and never returned. My mom hasn't seen her either. Grady, she could be anywhere."

"Did something happen to upset her?" Grady asked.

"Not that I know of."

"All right, go. We've got this," Grady said.

Patrick turned to Jonathan. "You should stay here. With you on crutches, you'll just slow me down."

"I want to help," Jonathan said, but the look on his face said he knew Patrick was right.

"I know. I'll bring her back safe. It'd ease my mind if you looked after my mom and aunt, Sammy, Dixie and Frannie."

Jonathan nodded.

"Keep your cell handy," Patrick said before walking out the door.

"I'm really worried about Abby," Sammy said.

"Wherever she is, I'm sure she's fine," Dixie said as she took Sammy's hand in hers.

Frannie had the urge to comfort Sammy

239

as well, but knew it wasn't her place. "What's going on with Abby?" she asked.

"She didn't come home after school," Dixie said. "In fact, she left school early. No one's seen her since this morning."

"Oh, dear," Mrs. Houston said, her hand pressed to her lips. Her face had gone white, and she clutched her sister's hand.

"Maybe she went to the diner," Frannie suggested.

"She wasn't scheduled to work. Because of the meeting tonight, I let her have the night off so she could be at home with Sammy."

"I'm too old for a babysitter," Sammy complained, but the way he snuggled into his grandmother's side conflicted with his statement. This kind of storm would terrify anyone, especially a kid caught somewhere between being a boy and a teenager.

"Of course you are," Frannie said. "It took a lot of courage to come out in the storm to tell your father and Dixie that your sister didn't come home."

Dixie gave Frannie a look of appreciation for what she'd said. It was nice to see something other than wariness and mistrust in her eyes.

Nodding, Dixie said, "Frannie's right, but it was dangerous. If something happened to both you and your sister, I don't know what we'd do."

Sammy looked up at Dixie. "You think Abby's hurt, don't you?"

"No, I didn't say that," Dixie insisted.

"I'm sure, wherever Abby is, that she's fine," Frannie said.

Patrick's mother remained silent, her lips moving behind her fingertips as if she said a prayer.

Jonathan joined them, hopping on one leg. There were too many people to maneuver with crutches. Frannie looked behind him, but didn't see Patrick despite the fact that the two men had left together.

"What's going on?" Dixie asked.

"The sheriff and Blake are assessing the condition of the building and the situation outside, trying to make sure it's safe for us to leave."

"Where's Patrick?" The words came out before Frannie could stop them.

"He left to go look for Abby."

"Oh, dear," Patrick's mother repeated, her lips moving more rapidly now.

Frannie felt her heart lurch at the idea of Patrick putting himself in harm's way, but of course, he had to go look for his daughter. Still, it couldn't be safe. What if another tornado formed or another severe thunder-

241

storm came through?

"How are you doing, sport?" Jonathan asked Sammy.

Sammy stood. "I want to go with Daddy to help find Abby."

Jonathan squeezed Sammy's shoulder, reassuring him while keeping him from rushing off. "I understand, dude. I wanted to go, too, but your daddy asked us to stay here to look after the womenfolk. I mean, we can't just leave them alone, right?"

Frannie and Dixie shared a look. They hadn't needed looking after since they'd left middle school, but they'd both let Sammy think they did if that kept him here and safe. Dixie shifted her gaze to Jonathan, giving him a softer version of the look she'd just shared with Frannie. The two clearly had feelings for each other, but so much stood between them. Dixie would be devastated when she learned that her best friend had had feelings for Jonathan, and that she'd had his baby. Keeping that secret for all these years had done so much damage. All those years of Patrick being in a loveless marriage, Abby not knowing her real father, Jonathan not knowing his daughter. There would have been hurt in the beginning, but these lifelong friends would have worked it out, just as they would now. But first, they had to find Abby.

"All right, folks," Grady was saying, "I need you to exit the building through the rear door. Please be cautious as there is a lot of debris outside the building. And prepare yourself for what you are about to see. A tornado has touched down in Angel Ridge."

CHAPTER 12

The devastation Patrick found when he stood on the courthouse lawn took his breath away. The fading light of the setting sun cast an eerie glow over the destruction. The roof of the courthouse had crushed several buildings on Main Street. Town Square looked like it had been plowed up. The gazebo was gone, and all the trees lay on their sides, uprooted. The only thing that stood untouched was the angel monument.

The roofs on several buildings had gaping holes and a lot of shingles missing, windows were broken, merchandise gone. Rain pelted him as he stepped over tree limbs and debris. The going was slow, but he picked his way along carefully, determined to make it to Ridge Road and then to his house in hope of finding Abby.

When he finally made it to the road, he found that the first few houses were gone. One had been owned by the town's librarian. The other had belonged to Grady's uncle and aunt who owned the grocery. All had, thankfully, been at the meeting. The next several houses were untouched, but then the next house no longer had a front porch. And it went on like that. Some houses were fine, while others had sustained various amounts of damage.

He moved as quickly as he could, praying his house still stood and that Abby was in it. As he approached the end of the road, he saw the devastation, and his heart stopped.

Frannie walked slowly outside with everyone else leaving the courthouse, or what was left of it. As they reached Main Street and Town Square, no one could speak, least of all Frannie. The tornado had ripped the roof off the courthouse, and it now sat squarely on what used to be the buildings that she had just bought for the Foundation. Parts of the roofs on other buildings were missing, windows broken, metal street lamps lay on the ground twisted, and the smell of natural gas burned her nose . . . it was too much to take in. So they all stood together at the end of Main, on the debris-riddled lawn of the courthouse, and stared.

Miss Estelee moved first. She went straight to the angel monument. Untouched, the warrior angel stood sentinel amid all the destruction, hands on the hilt of his sword, its tip resting between his sandaled feet. With a hand on the brick pedestal, Miss Estelee bent and pulled debris away from its base, all the while sending looks up at the angel above her.

Candi followed Miss Estelee. Not knowing what else to do, Frannie went as well.

"Miss Estelee? Leave that," Candi said. "There's broken glass everywhere. You could hurt yourself."

"He watched over us all," Miss Estelee said, her voice shaky and weak. "We're still here."

Frannie heard the words, wishing she could be as sure. Abby . . . She prayed the young girl was now safe in her father's arms.

"Yes," Candi agreed. "Guardian angels, an army of them, watched over us tonight." She rested her hands on Miss Estelee's shoulders. "Let's see about getting you home. Can I walk with you?"

Miss Estelee patted Candi's hand. "Yes. Yes, I would like to go home." She kissed her fingertips and touched them to the angel. "Thank you," she whispered, her eyes filling with tears. "Thank you."

Frannie watched them walk away, not sure what to do or where to go. People were milling around with stunned expressions. She saw Dixie, Jonathan, Patrick's mother and Sammy walking toward the diner, which looked undamaged. When she got her feet moving, she turned toward Ridge Road and home. The destruction seemed to be the worst nearest to town. Houses she'd passed on her way into town every morning since she'd moved to Angel Ridge, in just a few moments had disappeared. Everywhere she looked, she saw pieces of people's homes. Pictures that had once hung on walls were now lodged in trees along with clothing and other treasures.

When she turned to walk the rest of the way to her house, Patrick stood in her path. Without thinking, she walked straight into his arms. He held her tightly, and Frannie squeezed her eyes shut, not wanting to see anymore. And then she remembered. "Abby." She looked at Patrick. "Did you check your house? Was she there?"

Patrick had the same desperate, frightened expression he must be seeing when he looked at her. In answer, he just shook his head.

"Your house, is it still there?" she said softly.

He nodded, squeezing her arms.

"Okay, then we just have to keep searching. We'll find her, Patrick." She realized she was talking a lot while Patrick didn't speak. Still, she couldn't seem to stem the flow of words. "You know, I saw her the other day up in the Tall Pines. She said she liked to go there to sit when she had breaks at the diner. Maybe she's there. Have you checked there?"

"Frannie," his voice broke as he was saying her name.

"Don't tell me you found her and, and she's —"

"It's not that. It's just —"

"Stop, Patrick. We need to find your daughter." She took his hand and started walking back toward town and the road that led up to the Tall Pines.

"But Frannie . . ."

Whatever he had to say, if it was bad news, she did not want to hear it. Not now. "No 'buts.' Abby needs you. This town needs you. First, we have to make sure everyone is all right. This," she waved her hand at all the debris, "can be cleaned up. Things can be replaced. Anything else can wait. Right?"

He squeezed her hand. "You said 'we.'"

She nodded. "We all have to work together."

Suddenly, he wrapped her in the tightest, most comforting hug she'd ever experienced. It felt so right and natural to be in his arms — to stand with him at this moment. It felt like they could face this, and maybe anything else, together.

"Thank you," he whispered against her ear, smoothing a hand down her hair.

She could have stayed right there in Patrick's arms, on the sidewalk on Ridge Road for hours, but they didn't have that luxury. So she pushed against his chest. "Let's go get your daughter."

As they walked together toward the road at the end of Main that led up into the Tall Pines, Frannie was happy she'd chosen low wedges to wear with her business suit, still, jeans and tennis shoes would be much more practical for this. She unbuttoned her jacket. At his house, Patrick had picked up flashlights and tucked them into a backpack. He'd also changed into jeans and hiking shoes. She should have continued on to her house and changed, too, before she insisted they go up to the Tall Pines. She could be much more helpful in something other than a designer suit. As soon as they found Abby, she'd double back.

When they reached the top of the road that opened up into the clearing surrounded by tall pine trees, Frannie was breathing heavily.

Patrick pointed the flashlight in all directions. "Abby! Abby, are you here, honey?"

Ignoring the stitch in her side, Frannie walked to the spot where she'd seen Abby before. Some branches had fallen from the trees, so she dug through the pine needles and small branches littering the ground. "Abby? It's Frannie Thompson. I'm with your dad. Abby?"

She thought she saw a movement, but couldn't be sure. She shined her flashlight in that direction. "Patrick!" She kept digging, clearing out brush until she found a sneaker in her hand. Abby's sneaker. "Over here, Patrick!" She heard a moan. "Abby? Honey, it's okay. Your dad and I are here."

Abby tried to sit up, but fell back.

"Don't try to move. It's okay," Frannie said.

Patrick took Frannie's place. "I'm here, honey." He removed the rest of the brush covering Abby. "I'm here, honey," he repeated. "You're okay. You're okay," he said over and over.

When he tried to get his arms under her to lift her up, Frannie held him back. "You shouldn't move her. She could have broken bones."

He looked at her. "Right. Go see if you can find Doc Ferguson or Doc Prescott —"

"No." She was exhausted and afraid she'd never make it up the hill again. "You go. You're much faster than me. I'll stay with her."

"Daddy? I hurt all over."

Patrick brushed back his daughter's dark bangs from her forehead. "I know, honey. I'm going to get help."

"Don't leave me, Daddy. I was so afraid here all by myself. The sounds were awful, and then the trees started falling on me —"

"It's okay. Frannie will stay with you, and I'll be right back. I promise." He kissed her forehead. "I love you." And then he was gone.

Frannie scooted as close to Abby as she could, took her hand and smoothed her hair. Tears made lines in the dirt streaking the girl's face. "*Shh,* it's okay. You're not alone anymore."

"I was so scared."

"I know."

Frannie had been on her own so long, she knew how it felt. If a tornado had struck the condo she'd lived in before she moved to Angel Ridge, she would have died alone. It would have been days before anyone would have realized she was missing. In the few weeks she'd been in Angel Ridge, it had been nice to belong, to have people on the street smile and greet her by name. That had never happened in the city. The truth of the matter was she'd liked the anonymity, but something had changed since she'd come to Angel Ridge.

"Frannie? Is everyone okay? Sammy!" Frannie could hear the panic in Abby's voice. "I was supposed to watch him tonight."

"He's fine. He came to the Town Meeting when you didn't come home. Your dad has been looking for you ever since he realized you were missing. There was no way he wasn't finding you."

"But you found me, didn't you," Abby said. "You remembered that I told you I like to come here."

"Don't fret, Abby. All that matters is that you're safe now."

She squeezed Frannie's hand. "Everything's not okay. Nothing's ever going to be okay again."

Quiet sobs wracked Abby's body, and Frannie wanted to hold her so badly. Instead, she lay down beside her, as close as she could, and put an arm around her. "Don't cry, Abby. It's all going to be all right. As long as you have people who love and care about you, everything else will work itself out. Houses can be repaired and rebuilt. And besides, your dad has been to your house. He said it was fine."

She choked on a sob. "I don't care about the house."

Abby grabbed Frannie's blazer then, clutching the lapels. "I can't go back there. Don't make me go back. I don't want to."

Frannie grasped Abby's forearms. "What are you talking about, Abby? Of course we're taking you home. Where else would you go? You're hurt. You need your family, and they need you. They were all worried sick."

"They lied to me."

"What?"

"My whole life, they lied to me."

Frannie absorbed the meaning of that statement. Had Abby somehow found out Patrick wasn't her father? Was that why she hadn't returned to school? Why she'd been hiding up here in the Tall Pines?

"Over here," Patrick's voice rang out in the clearing, and then he was crouching beside Frannie and Abby.

"That was quick," Frannie said, sitting up so he could get to his daughter.

"Teams of emergency personnel are filling Town Square. I nabbed Janice and two EMTs with a stretcher. How is she?"

"Fine. Maybe in shock? I don't know,"

Frannie said. She stood, pulling Patrick back with her, so Dr. Ferguson could get in the tight space to examine Abby. "Let's give them room to work."

Patrick came with her reluctantly.

"Patrick," she began, with a hand at his arm. "I think I know why Abby went missing today."

He swung his worried gaze from Abby to Frannie. "Did she say something?"

Nodding, Frannie said, "She said she didn't want to go home because she'd been lied to. She said something about being lied to her whole life."

"Oh God . . ." Patrick breathed.

"Do you think someone could have told her about Jonathan?" Frannie asked.

"I don't know. Who would do that? I mean, I talked to Jonathan about this earlier today, and we agreed to wait to tell her."

"Could she have overheard?"

"Patrick," Janice said joining them, "I think we need to transfer Abby to the hospital for x-rays. She's favoring her side and may have some strained or broken ribs. I also suspect she has a concussion. She's complaining about her hip and leg, all left side. She doesn't seem to remember what happened, but it looks like she took a pretty bad fall."

"She'll be okay, though, right?" Patrick said.

Janice squeezed his arm. "We'll know more after we get her to the hospital. I'm going to ask them to take her to the University of Tennessee ER. They have a better trauma center. With the destruction in town, we should have her air lifted. I think Lifestar could land in this clearing, don't you?"

"Yeah. That should work for anyone who's injured and needs to go to the emergency room. Good thinking," Patrick said.

Janice pulled a two-way radio out of her bag. "Good thing Grady gave me this since cell phone service is down."

"He's done an amazing job managing this," Patrick said, admiring his friend's preparedness.

Janice radioed paramedics below, requesting airlift and asking them to instruct the chopper to land in the clearing at the Tall Pines above town. Patrick returned to his daughter, kneeling beside her. "How are you doing, sweetie?"

Abby sniffed, but didn't answer.

"Doc Ferguson thinks you need to go to the hospital for x-rays. They're going to take you in a helicopter. With the roads blocked by trees and debris from the tornado, it's the best and quickest way to get you there."

"I want Dixie to go with me."

Surprised, Patrick said, "I'm not sure where Dixie is. It might take too much time to find her. I'll go with you."

"No," Abby said flatly. At that one word, Patrick looked as if he'd been stabbed in the heart.

"Frannie?" Abby said.

"Yes, Abby. I'm here," Frannie said from behind them.

"Would you go with me to the hospital?"

Frannie looked from Abby's pleading eyes and tear-streaked face to Patrick. He closed his eyes and nodded, clearly hurting from his daughter's rejection. Dear Lord, how she hated hospitals, but how could she say "no"?

"Of course I'll go with you."

The girl swiped at her cheeks with the back of her hand.

"If you folks could give us some room, we need to get her loaded onto a backboard."

Patrick took Frannie's arm and guided her back toward the clearing.

"I'm sorry," Frannie said, squeezing his hand.

"I'll get there as soon as I can."

"Of course. I'll call you when we know more about Abby."

A muscle ticked in Patrick's jaw. He pulled out his wallet and handed her an insurance card.

"They need you here, too," Frannie added.

"Yeah, we're going to have to set up a temporary shelter at the school. I'll have to coordinate with Grady and the Red Cross, get those who are able to help out."

"Right," Frannie agreed. "She'll be fine. UT is an excellent hospital."

"Bruises and bones will heal, thank God. But the rest . . . she may never forgive me. I can't lose my little girl, too, Frannie."

She touched his face. "You won't. She's just shocked and upset. When that passes, she'll be ready to listen to what you have to say. Just be there for her, Patrick. That's all you can do right now."

"If she'll let me," he said, regret lacing his words.

The whir of helicopter blades had them both looking up as the orange and white medical aircraft circled the clearing, familiarizing itself with the terrain before landing. Janice met the EMTs and gave them a rundown of Abby's condition. The man and woman who'd come up to the clearing with Janice had Abby strapped to a board. Before they lifted and carried her to the chopper, Patrick went to his daughter.

He smoothed a hand over her hair then wiped the tears that still fell from her cheeks. "I love you, honey. I'll come to the hospital as soon as I can."

"You don't have to," she said.

Frannie could tell Abby desperately wanted her father, but was too stubborn to admit it.

"Of course I do," he insisted. "You're my daughter. I love you."

Frannie choked back tears of her own when he leaned in to press a lingering kiss on Abby's forehead.

"I love you," he repeated. "I'm so proud of how brave you're being. I know how much you must be hurting."

Frannie didn't know if he was talking about her injuries, her emotional pain, or both.

"No matter what, I'll always be your daddy, and I'll always love you," he promised.

"We should take her now," Janice said.

They carried Abby the rest of the way to the helicopter. Frannie followed. As she looked back at Patrick, she could have sworn she heard Abby say, "I love you, too, Daddy."

CHAPTER 13

Patrick spent a long night doing his best to help coordinate disaster relief efforts in Angel Ridge. As the sun came up behind Lake Tellassee, which sat below the ridge, people could be seen stopping what they were doing just to look in disbelief at the damage caused by the tornado. News crews had arrived before sunrise to televise live from Town Square. All of the reporters from the various stations had requested an interview.

Road crews had worked all night to clear at least one route into town. The Red Cross had set up a shelter and command post in the school. Everyone in town was accounted for. A few people had been hurt, but thankfully, with most people at the Town Hall Meeting last night, the injuries had been minor and minimal, with Abby being hurt the worst. If they'd waited five more minutes to get everyone down to the jail in the basement of the building, it would have been an entirely different story.

Frannie had called a few hours ago to let him know she'd spoken to a doctor who'd told her Abby had a mild concussion, two broken ribs, a sprained ankle and numerous scrapes and bruises. The worst injury was that one of her broken ribs had punctured her spleen. They were doing more tests to determine if it should be removed.

Patrick needed to get to the hospital, and he would, as soon as he finished some last minute organizational details in town. He approached the diner to find Cole Craig, Grady Wallace and Blake Ferguson waiting outside.

"Thank you for meeting me," Patrick said. "I know you all must be exhausted."

"We're fine," Cole said. "How's Abby?"

"Resting. They're still running tests, and I need to get to the hospital."

"Of course," Blake agreed. "What can we do to help here so you can go?"

Patrick couldn't have better friends than these men. They'd grown up together, and he loved them like brothers. He'd loved Jonathan the same way, and Dixie and Susan had been like the sisters he never had. Times were simpler and uncomplicated then. The biggest decision they'd had to make was deciding whose house they'd hang out at after school.

"Blake, I need you and Cole to coordinate the cleanup efforts. There will be volunteers and county road crews in town soon. The utility crews will also be working night and day to restore power and phone service. I've let county officials know that you are the go-to guys if I can't be reached. I hope that was okay."

"Of course," Cole and Blake said in unison.

"Grady, the television crews want interviews. If you could handle that, I think I might be able to leave."

"No problem. Go," Grady said.

"Doc Ferguson and Doc Prescott asked if Candi could lend a hand at the clinic today," Patrick said. "I'm not sure if she got the message."

"She's already there," Grady confirmed. "They didn't have to keep anyone overnight, but they're ready if more people with injuries come in today."

"Good." He paused, torn between wanting to leave and needing to talk to Jonathan first.

"Is there something else?" Grady asked.

"Have any of you seen Jonathan?"

"He's with Dixie in the diner," Blake said.

261

"They're making sack lunches. He wanted to help, but with his knee, there wasn't a lot he could do. So he's back in the kitchen, sitting on a stool, making sandwiches."

Patrick nodded. "I'll just have a word with him and be on my way."

"Don't worry about anything here. We've got this."

"Thanks, guys, I can't tell you —" He broke off, unable to put his feelings into words.

Grady clapped him on the shoulder. "We know."

Swallowing hard against the lump of emotion in his throat, he turned and walked into the diner. It was deserted with everyone out in town doing what they could to help.

"Patrick," Dixie said as he walked into the kitchen, "how's Abby?"

Jonathan stopped what he was doing, wiped his hands on a towel, and stood.

"Jonathan, how are you doing? How's your leg?" Patrick asked.

"Fine. How's Abby?" he said, repeating Dixie's question.

He relayed what Frannie had told him. "I'm just leaving for the hospital now. They should know something soon about whether or not her spleen can be saved."

"Did Abby say what happened when you

262

found her?" Dixie asked.

"She couldn't seem to remember. When she fell, she hit her head." He paused, not sure if he should say more in front of Dixie. It had been Susan's dearest wish that Dixie never know about Susan's mistake with Jonathan. But that lie had affected so many lives.

Jonathan glanced over at Dixie, then said to Patrick, "I'll walk you to the door. Be right back, Dixie."

In an uncharacteristic move, Dixie hugged Patrick hard. Sniffed and then stepped back. "Give Abby my love, and call to let us know what's going on."

"Of course," Patrick promised. "Be sure and pace yourself, Dix. Try and get a nap in if you can. Both of you," he said to Jonathan as well. "None of us will be able to help anyone if we're dropping from exhaustion."

Neither argued, surprising Patrick again. Dixie typically would never admit to weakness, but in this kind of life-altering situation, the ground had shifted beneath them, removing their stability. Before leaving the kitchen, he leaned down and kissed Dixie's cheek.

She swatted at him with the back of her hand. "Get out of here," she said and quickly turned away, but not before he saw her swipe away a tear.

Jonathan followed Patrick to the front of the diner and didn't waste time before saying, "What's going on? What couldn't you say in front of Dixie?"

"She knows. Abby knows I'm not her biological father."

"What?" Jonathan bit out quietly. "How could that happen?"

"I'm not sure, but she told Frannie she didn't want to come home because she'd been lied to her entire life." He paused while Jonathan absorbed that. "She didn't want me to go to the hospital with her."

"Who could have told her? No one knows but the two of us, right?"

"Right," Patrick said, not counting Frannie who clearly hadn't said anything. "Abby left school yesterday morning to get her book bag. If she left it here, she might have overheard us talking."

Jonathan rubbed his eyes. "How are you going to handle it with her?"

"I'm going to be honest." He lifted his chin toward the kitchen. "You might want to do the same."

Frannie woke with the feeling of someone caressing her cheek and hair. When she opened her eyes, she looked into another pair of eyes the color of a clear sky after the rain.

"Hi," Patrick said.

"Hi."

She let the recliner down and sat up. Because Abby was in the intensive care unit, Frannie had spent the night in this waiting room with a number of other families who had been negatively affected by last night's storms.

"How are you?" Patrick asked.

"Me? Don't you want to ask about Abby first?"

"I just saw her. I stopped by the nurse's desk. The doctor was in with her, so they let me go back."

Instantly alert, Frannie asked, "What did the doctor say?"

"They're prepping her for surgery."

"Oh, no."

"The doctor is sure she'll be fine," Patrick said.

"I'm sorry, Patrick."

"Me, too." He paused, but didn't stop looking at her. Taking her hand, he said, "Thank you for being here for her."

"I'm sorry that she didn't want you to come. I could see how that hurt you last night."

265

He shrugged. "I have to accept responsibility for that. I helped create the situation." He rubbed some warmth into her cold hands. "Did she say anything else last night?"

"No. They gave her some pretty heavy medication to control her pain. So she slept through most of the night, I think. At least, when I saw her, she was sleeping. But I held her hand and talked to her so she would know she wasn't alone."

"Thank you for that."

They sat there quietly for a moment, and then Patrick chuckled.

"What?" she said.

"It's not fair. You even look good in someone else's scrubs."

Frannie glanced at the blue cotton shirt and pants. "A nurse gave them to me last night. She even had tennis shoes in her gym bag that she let me borrow."

"You look wonderful."

She doubted that. Inky shadows marred the skin beneath his eyes, and she touched her fingertips to his cheek. "How are you? How is the town? Was anyone else injured?"

Patrick took her hand and kissed her palm. "I'm a little tired, but fine. Miraculously, there were only minor injuries. Everyone in town is accounted for. A lot of businesses were damaged, and people have lost their homes, but everyone is working together to help those with the most need."

"Where did those people stay last night?" Frannie asked. Patrick didn't respond. When the silence lengthened, she asked, "What is it, Patrick? What aren't you telling me?"

"Some of the people who lost their homes stayed at a shelter we set up at the school."

"Some?" He brought her hand to his lips and gently kissed the back of her fingers. "Patrick, you're scaring me. Just say it."

Holding her gaze, he spoke softly. "Frannie, your house, it was destroyed."

"Oh," she said in a rush, a hundred different emotions fighting for attention inside her — shock, disbelief, relief and thankfulness that she hadn't been there. But, still, "Jenny's house is gone?"

"Yes."

"Okay," she nodded, trying to understand, but somehow unable to. The last tangible thing connecting her to her sister was gone. The buildings that would hold her new business *and* her sister's house, her home, were all gone. Everything that tied her to Angel Ridge was gone. She couldn't process it, so she said, "You're tired. Here, take the chair and have a nap. I'll go down and get

267

some coffee. Are you hungry? I can grab something to eat and bring it back."

She stood, but Patrick didn't release her hand. "Stop. Sit."

"I've been sitting all night."

"I'm not asking you to sit because you need to. I'm asking you to sit because you're upset. I know you saw your property on Main when you left the courthouse last night, and now I've told you your home is gone, too. It's not exactly a coffee and food moment." He paused, looking up at her, then added, "If you think I'm going to sleep after telling you something so devastating, you don't know me very well."

In an attempt at humor, she said, "Well, I've been saying that all along, but you wouldn't hear it." She allowed him to pull her back to sit on the edge of the recliner.

"I've tried to rectify the situation."

"I'd say improvements have been made in that arena."

"I don't want you to worry," Patrick said softly. "You'll have somewhere to stay."

Frannie turned away. "Please, Patrick. I can't think about that right now. I just can't."

"Okay. But when you're ready, we'll deal with it together."

"Patrick, it's not realistic for you to say

that, not with your daughter in the hospital and having major surgery. Add to that the situation with you, her, and Jonathan, and the town being in shambles. You have much more than you could possibly handle at the moment without taking on my circumstances, too."

"Stop," he said sharply.

"What?"

"Don't you dare pull away now. I need you." He leaned in, his face so close she could feel his breath on her lips. "We need each other. I know our relationship, if you can call it that, has barely gotten off the ground, but . . ." He cupped her cheek before continuing, "I'm not sure I can get through this without you, Frannie. And if you'll let me, I'll be there for you, too. I want that. I hope you want the same."

He was right, of course, but she refused to think about the two of them as a unit. Even though she'd been warming to the idea, she still couldn't do it. But Patrick was right. Bailing on her new home and her new friends at such a difficult time would be wrong. She should go back to Angel Ridge and do everything she could to help her neighbors put their lives back together. But at the end of the day, where would she go? How could her life be reassembled? She'd been in town only a short time. It would be so easy to take this as a sign, cut her losses and go back home to Nashville. Any rational person would do just that.

However, sitting so close to Patrick, touching him, looking into his eyes while he looked back at her, opened up a gaping hole inside her heart she wanted him to fill. As usual, she was afraid to hope. Good things didn't happen for her. Things never worked out the way she wanted. Why should she have expected anything different when she made this move? Clearly, it had been a colossal mistake.

Putting her hand over his and leaning into his touch, she closed her eyes and allowed herself a moment to accept his comfort — a moment to imagine what loving someone like Patrick, and having that love returned, could be like. When she opened her eyes, the bright morning light shining through the tall windows of the sterile room shattered the image like the most fragile crystal.

"I'm here," she said. She couldn't promise him tomorrow, but she could give him now.

Patrick woke some time later, with the sun still streaming through the windows of the large room. It was a big area, filled with generic chairs and vinyl-covered recliners.

Groups of people huddled together, waiting for hourly visits with their loved ones.

The phone rang and someone answered, then called out, "Anderson family?"

He wondered if there'd been any calls about Abby while he'd slept. Where was Frannie? He searched the room, but she wasn't there.

He stood, straightened his wrinkled clothing and was about to go to the nurse's station to enquire about Abby when Dixie came into the room.

She glanced around, and seeing him, walked over to where he stood. "How is she?"

"They took her to surgery earlier. We haven't heard anything yet. I was just about to go get an update."

"Well, don't let me stop you. I'll be here when you get back."

He looked for Frannie on his way to the nurses' desk, but didn't see her. The nurse, whose nametag read Sandra, confirmed that Abby was still in surgery and that the nurses on the surgical floor would call as soon as they could. So, he retraced his steps to the waiting area. Dixie stood in the same spot where he'd left her, but still, no Frannie.

"They said she's still in surgery."

"That's it?"

271

"They'll call this room when she's in recovery," Patrick said.

"So, hurry up and wait, basically."

He checked his watch. "Yeah." He'd been asleep for about four hours. "Where's Sammy?"

"With your mom," Dixie said. "It wasn't easy talking him into staying. He wanted to come with me. I think your mom has aged ten years since last night."

He knew the feeling. "I'll call them when Abby gets out of surgery." Patrick jammed his hands into his pockets. "Can you stay for a little while?"

"I plan to stay until I can see Abby," Dixie confirmed.

Now that he took a closer look at Dixie, he could see she was a bit pale and her eyes were puffy. "Let's sit then." He pulled a chair around close so she could sit and they could speak privately. "How are things going in town?"

"As well as can be expected," she said flatly, not elaborating.

He couldn't remember a time when Dixie did not elaborate, but he played along. "Is the power back on?"

"No. They're saying that might take awhile. Like, a week, maybe two."

"Wow."

"I knew it was bad, but seeing it all in the light of day . . ."

He chanced squeezing her hand. The fact she let him said a lot. "I know." After a pause, Patrick ventured in. "How are you, Dixie?"

She swung her gaze to his, unable to hide the pain straining her features and filling her dark eyes. "You mean, how are you now that you know your best friend lied to you all of your adult life? Not great."

"So, Jonathan told you."

"Yes, he told me that the three of you conspired to keep this horrific secret from me in order to spare my feelings."

It would be hard for her to hear, but it needed saying. "It's what Susan asked of us. She hated what she'd done. More than anything, she didn't want to hurt you."

"Yeah, Jonathan explained how he planned to tell me the truth from the beginning but Susan convinced him otherwise." She laughed, a painful sound that could just as easily have been a sob, but no tears fell. "I can almost understand that, but the reasoning was faulty from the beginning. I didn't need to be protected from the truth then, or in all the years since. Of course I would have been devastated, but if I'd been told then, I could have had it out with Susan.

I'm sorry, but it just ticks me off that she's gone and I can't even say what I need to say to her."

"I understand," Patrick said. Dixie had every right to her anger.

"What I don't understand is how you got mixed up in all of this, Patrick."

He nodded, staring at his hands. "At the time, I thought it was the right thing to do. Susan was in a bad spot, and I wanted to help." He looked up at Dixie. "I would have done the same for you."

"The difference being, I never would have been in that spot."

"Don't judge them too harshly, Dix."

"I'll judge them as harshly as I'd like. My best friend had drunken sex with my boyfriend the night of the prom while you and I," she wagged a finger between the two of them, "were at home in bed with the flu."

"Susan wasn't drunk," he corrected.

"Oh," she threw her hands up and waved them around, "that makes it so much better. She *knew* she was screwing my boyfriend."

That drew a few glances from a few people sitting close by, but Patrick ignored it. Dixie had a right to yell and stomp and rave a little.

"Susan had feelings for him, Dix. She

fought them for years, for your sake, but she was human. In a weak moment, she lost control and made a mistake. One she regretted for the rest of her life."

"Damn it to hell, she should have told me, Patrick. She should have told me all of it."

"I know. Come here." He opened his arms, and Dixie leaned in, laying her head on his shoulder. He could feel her tears soaking his shirt while he held her head and rubbed her back.

"I'm sorry," she whispered brokenly.

"Don't be."

She leaned back and swiped at her tears, trying to pull it together. "It's just too much at once. The tornado, Abby . . . I had just begun to let myself trust Jonathan again. He seemed so sincere in his apologies when he got back to town. So determined to show me that this time would be different." She sniffed. "But that's my fault. How could I have even considered giving him yet another chance?"

"He's wanted to tell Abby for awhile now. I convinced him to wait. She's been having such a hard time since Susan died."

"Things were getting better with her," Dixie said.

"And now this."

"How do you want to handle it?" Dixie

asked Patrick.

He rested his elbows on his knees and linked his hands. "She knows. All I can do is answer her questions truthfully and apologize."

"Are you going to tell her it was her mom who insisted on keeping the secret all these years?"

"I can't put all the blame on Susan. We were all complicit in the lie, all of us except for you."

"Who else knows? Blake? Cole? Grady?"

"Just the three of us," he hesitated, then added, "and I told Frannie."

"You care about her, don't you?" Dixie asked.

"Yes." No point in denying it.

Dixie sucked in a breath then and leaned back, like something had just occurred to her. "Your drinking . . . It was because of this, wasn't it?"

"I chose to drink," Patrick said. "I won't lay the blame for that anywhere but with myself."

"But you were living a lie. You didn't love Susan, did you?"

"I loved her the way I always had — as a friend. I wanted to love her that way. I tried, but my feelings for her never evolved into anything more."

"And she knew."

"Of course."

"Which made you feel guilty."

Patrick nodded.

"Did she ever love you that way?" Dixie asked.

"She said she did, but I don't think she ever got over Jonathan."

Dixie reacted swiftly to that revelation. "How could she do this?" she asked. "In the process of her working so hard to not hurt me, she hurt you and Jonathan instead." She turned away, chewing on her thumbnail. "And now Abby."

"I wanted to tell Abby. I begged Susan to reconsider and tell our daughter the truth. But she refused."

It was Dixie's turn to squeeze his hands now. "You are her father, Patrick, in every way that matters."

"I haven't been there for her. My drinking and my own conflicted feelings about not being her father got in the way. I always felt like I was cheating her, trying to be a stand-in dad when she could have known her real father. She deserved to know him. And now, she and Jonathan have lost eighteen years they can never get back."

"Don't be so hard on yourself."

"Why not?" Patrick demanded. "I went

along. If I hadn't married Susan, the truth would have come to light when Jonathan figured it out."

"Her father would have killed her. You know she didn't have the most stable home life."

"I know. That was the main reason I married her. I was afraid of her father's reaction when he found out she'd gotten pregnant." He rubbed the stubble lining his jaw. "In my eighteen-year-old mind, it was the only way I could figure to keep her safe."

"What a mess," Dixie said.

"I'm sorry, Dixie. We all made mistakes in this. I hope that someday, you can forgive us."

"I don't blame you, Patrick. What you did was noble."

Frannie had said much the same thing, but he couldn't see how living a lie was noble. "Thank you for that," he said. "What about Susan and Jonathan?"

"I'm just beginning to process all this. Don't expect me to forgive and forget quickly," Dixie said.

"Of course. You need time." Patrick shifted his gaze to the door, wondering what had happened to Frannie.

"Looking for someone?"

"Frannie. She came to the hospital with

Abby and was here when I arrived. But I fell asleep and haven't seen her since I woke up."

"I have to say this. When we had that snowstorm back when all that went down with Jenny and Candi, something happened between you and Frannie, didn't it?"

Since this seemed to be the day for honesty, he said, "I ran into her in a bar outside of town in the middle of that snowstorm. You were staying with Susan that night." He paused, feeling the regret pull at him even now. "We kissed. She didn't know I was married."

"You were drunk," Dixie supplied.

"That's no excuse."

"She realized you were married because of something I said the next morning in the diner."

Patrick nodded.

"But she's been able to move past that now?"

"I hope so. I've been honest about everything with her. Don't get me wrong, she gave me hell about it," Patrick added.

"As well she should."

"I hope she understands that one mistake, or even a series of them, doesn't necessarily define a person, especially if they're trying to make amends for those mistakes."

279

Dixie's eyebrows rose toward her hairline. "I suppose there's some hidden meaning in there for me to consider where Susan and Jonathan are concerned?"

"I'm just happy that Frannie might be giving me a chance to show her the real me, the sober me. What you decide to do about Jonathan is between you and him."

"And what do I do about Susan?" Dixie asked.

"Whatever you need to say can still be said. Just know this, what she did, she did because of how much she loved you. When the anger burns off —"

"*If* it burns off," Dixie inserted.

"I hope you'll find that the love is still there."

After several moments had passed, Dixie said, "I have a confession to make, Patrick."

He didn't speak. Just waited.

"For a lot of years, I felt like you didn't treat Susan right. I think I knew all along that you didn't love her, that maybe you just married her because she was pregnant."

"I know," Patrick said.

"And you took it, knowing all along —"

"Yes. I could deal with you hating me as long as you and Susan had each other. She needed you, Dixie."

Dixie swallowed hard but met his eyes

when she said, "I misjudged you, and I'm sorry. I hope you can forgive me."

The phone in the waiting room rang, and someone stood to go answer it.

Patrick smiled. "I'd like for us to be friends again."

"I'd like that, too," Dixie admitted. "But don't get me wrong," she wagged a finger at him, "that doesn't mean I'm going to take it easy on you."

Chuckling, Patrick said, "You wouldn't be the Dixie we all love if you did."

"Houston family?" someone said.

"Here," Patrick answered, going to the phone. "Hello, this is Patrick Houston."

"This is recovery. Your daughter is out of surgery. We'll bring her down to ICU in thirty minutes to an hour."

"How is she?"

"The surgery went well. Your daughter should make a full recovery."

Patrick hung up the phone, and then went to Dixie, lifting her from her chair to swing her around in a circle.

"What in the world?" Dixie said, when he set her back on her feet.

"Abby's out of surgery. She's going to be all right!"

"Thank you, Jesus," Dixie said, hugging

281

Patrick. "That's a fine start to turning a whole lot of bad into some good."

CHAPTER 14

"Frannie? It's Janice Ferguson. How are you?"

Frannie held the phone to her ear as she paced the hallway of the hospital. "Fine. Are you calling about my blood work?"

"Yes, that and to let you know how sorry I am about your house."

"Thank you." *Why wasn't Janice telling her about the test results?*

"I have a supply of your prescriptions here. I ordered them after you came to see me. So, come by anytime today to pick them up, okay?"

"Sure." *Why was Janice delaying?* "Was my blood work okay?"

A beat of silence, and then Janice said, "It was inconclusive. Your blood cell count is a bit off, but not by much. Still, I'd like to err on the side of caution and run more tests."

Frannie froze at the doctor's words.

"Now, I don't want you to worry about

this until we know more. No need borrowing trouble," Janice said. "Are you still at the hospital?"

"Yes. Abby is in surgery. They had to remove her spleen."

"Yes, I've been in contact with her doctors, following the case even though I can't be there."

"Oh. Of course," Frannie said, upset about her irregular blood work.

"I've called the lab and requested the tests I want run. So go down and have your blood drawn, okay? They're located on the ground floor, near the lobby."

Frannie didn't answer, couldn't seem to find her voice.

"Frannie?"

"Yes," she said at last. "I'll go now."

"Good. Tell Patrick we're praying for Abby's speedy recovery."

"I will."

Frannie disconnected the call and took the elevator to the first floor of the hospital. Following the signs, she found the lab and signed in with the receptionist. She sat, numb, waiting to be called.

A half hour later, she called a cab and left the hospital. She couldn't stay in the sterile environment another minute without imagining herself there again.

Driving from Knoxville to Angel Ridge took three times as long as it normally would have. Everything had been fine until they'd gotten through Maryville. After that, a couple of miles before the turnoff on the road that led to Angel Ridge, traffic slowed to a crawl. The destruction lay out before her in endless piles of wood that had been houses. Uprooted trees lay on their sides, while mangled cars littered yards, and surprisingly, appliances sat undamaged miles from the kitchens they'd once occupied.

When she at last reached the road that would take her into Angel Ridge, a Blount County deputy stopped the cab. "I'm sorry, but this road is closed. Only residents can enter," he said to the driver.

Frannie leaned forward and said, "I live in Angel Ridge. I had to go to the hospital last night with a girl who was injured, so I don't have my car."

"Can I see some identification?"

Frannie got out of the cab, feeling odd wearing scrubs, and belatedly realized she didn't have any ID. "I'm afraid that in all the confusion last night, I left without my purse. You can call the sheriff in town. He'll verify that I live there."

"Naw. I trust you. You can go through."

The officer paused, then added, "I'm sorry for the losses the town has suffered, ma'am."

"Thank you," she said before getting back in the cab.

As they continued slowly forward, the damage took Frannie's breath away. On Ridge Road, things would look normal with houses untouched, just tree limbs down and other debris scattered about, and then there'd be a gaping hole where a house had once stood. The cab slowed, pulling up to the curb near her mailbox.

"Ma'am?" the cab driver said. "Is this your address?"

All Frannie could do was nod. She reached for her purse, then remembered. "I'm so sorry. I forgot that I don't have my wallet." With her home and everything in it gone, she had no way to get money.

The driver got out and held the door open. When she stood beside him, he said, "I couldn't take your money. I'm so sorry. Is there somewhere I can take you? Do you have a relative or friends that you can stay with?"

She shook her head, still unable to speak as she stared at the site where Jenny's home used to be.

"I don't feel right just leaving you here, ma'am."

"I'll be fine. Thank you . . . for your kindness," Frannie said.

The older man reluctantly got back into his cab and drove away. Frannie walked up the steps to the sidewalk that once led to her front porch. A fallen tree at the end of her driveway now impeded her progress, but that was okay since the sidewalk went nowhere now. The garage was gone, too, along with her car. The only thing left intact was the storage building in the back corner of the yard — the building that held the lawnmower Patrick had just fixed for her.

She turned in a slow circle, looking for anything that had been inside. Nothing. Not an article of clothing, a book, a picture, or piece of furniture remained. She walked across the concrete foundation to the backyard. A single red rose bloomed on one of the bushes that lined the fence between her house and Patrick's. So perfect, she had to touch it to convince herself it was real and not a figment of her imagination.

Her knees gave out then, and she crumpled to the ground. Though tears and shock clogged her throat, her eyes remained dry. Unaware of how long she sat there staring up at that rose, she finally stood on unsteady knees and moved slowly towards town. Several people greeted her along the way, asking if she was all right, if she needed anything. She nodded or shook her head with the appropriate response, still unable to find her voice.

When she reached town, she saw that most of the shops with holes in their roofs had attached bright blue tarps to protect the interiors from rain until repairs could be made. All of the debris in Town Square had been gathered into a neat pile, and someone with a bobcat was smoothing the surface of the lawn. The roof of the courthouse, lying on the buildings she had bought from Mr. DeFoe, drew her. She continued until she stood directly across from the strange sight.

"It's a sight, ain't it," someone said, giving words to her thoughts.

Frannie pushed her hair back from her face and looked around to see who had spoken. Miss Estelee sat on the bench near the angel monument, the same spot where she and Frannie had sat after that first meeting she'd had with Patrick.

Turning, she walked over to Miss Estelee.

"Rest yourself, dear. It's a lot to take in."

"Ms. Thompson!" Mrs. McKay had seen Frannie and made a beeline for where she sat with Miss Estelee. "Ms. Thompson, a word."

What could the woman possibly want at a time like this?

"I've been looking for you. I have something to say, and you're going to hear it," Mrs. McKay all but shouted.

"Settle down, Harriet," Miss Estelee said. "The girl's suffered as much loss as anyone in this. She don't need you heaping your ashes on her head."

"For once, would you just keep quiet, Estelee?"

"Harriet!" Mr. McKay boomed, trailing his wife's steps, trying to stop her.

"I'll thank you to show some respect for your elders, Harriet McKay. Your mamma taught you better!"

Ignoring that, Mrs. McKay swept a hand in the direction of the courthouse roof on Frannie's storefronts. "Do you see that? That is your answer, Ms. Thompson, to the question of whether or not your little venture belongs in Angel Ridge. And the punctuation mark is the fact that your home is gone, too."

"Harriet!" Mr. McKay said, grasping her arm.

The tall, thin lady's face was blotched red. Undeterred, she wrenched her arm free of her husband's grasp. "You have nowhere to go now except back where you came from."

Reverend Reynolds from the Presbyterian Church, hearing the disturbance, had joined them now. "Mrs. McKay, where is your Christian sense of compassion? Can't you see that Ms. Thompson is upset? Look at her. She's pale from shock. Why, she's been at the hospital all night looking after Abby Houston and, I'm sure, has only just returned to town to see the damage to her property."

Miss Estelee reached over and took Frannie's hand in both hers, while Frannie just sat there, the scene unfolding around her like she was watching a movie.

"You're a man of the cloth," Mrs. McKay said to Reverend Reynolds. "If this is not a sign, I am certain I do not know what is."

"That's nonsense, Mrs. McKay," the pastor said. "This is a tragedy, nothing more, nothing less. A difficulty that should have us coming together to help one another rather than tearing each other down."

"Right," Mr. McKay agreed, grasping Mrs. McKay's arm once again. With a firmer grip this time, he propelled her back across the Square toward the bank. "My apologies, Ms. Thompson."

"I'm not sorry!" Mrs. McKay's eyes were wild now with hysteria overtaking her. "You need to go!"

Mr. McKay pulled his wife close, saying something to her that none of them could hear. "So sorry," he repeated before they disappeared inside the bank.

The pastor knelt in front of Frannie. "Would you like me to walk you over to see the doctor, Frannie?"

Frannie shook her head.

Miss Estelee patted her hand. "We'll be fine, Preacher. Why don't you check back on us in a bit?"

Worry clearly etched Reverend Reynolds' face. "All right," he said, "but I'll be nearby if you need me."

After he'd walked away, Miss Estelee said, "Honey, look at me. Look into this old lady's eyes and take you some deep breaths."

Frannie swung her gaze to Miss Estelee's and stared into the old woman's soft blue eyes. As Frannie pulled in a few shaky breaths, she felt some of her panic ease. Still, Mrs. McKay's words rumbled around in her head.

"Now, you can't pay Harriet McKay no mind. She don't know what she's sayin'."

Frannie still didn't speak, but she kept her focus on Miss Estelee.

"Listen close, Frannie. I've got a word for you."

Frannie had no idea what that meant, but

listening seemed to be the only thing she could do at the moment.

"It's times like this that gets me to thinkin' about the scriptures, and I reckon Psalm 23 comes to mind. It says:

"The Lord is my Shepherd, I shall not want. He makes me to lie down in green pastures, he leads me beside the still waters, he restores my soul; He leads me in the paths of righteousness for His name's sake.

"Yea, though I walk through the valley of the shadow of death, I will fear no evil, For You are with me; Your rod and Your staff, they comfort me.

"You prepare a table before me in the presence of my enemies, You anoint my head with oil, My cup runs over.

"Surely goodness and mercy will follow me all the days of my life, and I will dwell in the house of the Lord forever."

"To me, that means that no matter how bad things get, whether it be loss of property, the people I love, or even my health, which eventually fails us all, dear, God is there with us, to comfort and keep us and give us everything we need. Even when enemies press in on all sides, He holds us in a place of honor. There might be some hard times to get through, but there's peace and love on the other side of it."

"I don't understand," Frannie said, her voice sounding like someone else's when she heard it.

"For one so young, I reckon you've seen more than your fair share of trouble."

"Yes," Frannie whispered.

"But here in Angel Ridge, you've gotten a glimpse of something beautiful, and you long to claim it for your own, right?"

Frannie bit down hard on her lower lip, afraid to speak the words out loud.

"Say what's in your heart," Miss Estelee encouraged, "because even though the good Lord knows what we want and what we need, He wants us to tell him anyway."

"I would like to stay in Angel Ridge," Frannie admitted, "but everything I had here has been destroyed. How can I stay now?" Especially if on top of all that, she was sick again.

"Everything?" Miss Estelee asked. "The way I see it, them buildings over there and your house was taken. Were they the reasons you wanted to stay here?"

After a moment, Frannie whispered, "No."

"So what was it here that made you want to stay?"

"The people," Frannie admitted.

"And a certain person in particular?" Miss Estelee pressed.

Frannie nodded again, but added, "It's wrong for me to want him."

"Why's that?"

"Because I've not been completely honest with him."

"Why not?"

Frannie thought about that for a minute. She'd convinced herself that she couldn't ask him to consider being with a cancer survivor given that he'd already lost a wife to the disease. But truthfully, the reason she hadn't told him about her illness was because she feared he would turn her away because of it. After living in Angel Ridge with these people and Patrick, she couldn't bear the thought of once again falling back into the isolation where she'd once found comfort.

"I'm afraid of rejection," she admitted.

"*Mmm-hmm.* Fear is something the evil one sends our way to separate folks from the happiness God intends for them. If we allow the fear to overtake us, then we got nobody to blame for our own unhappiness but ourselves. So, what are you going to do, Frannie Thompson? Are you going to reach out and grab hold of the happiness being offered to you, or will you choose fear and loneliness instead?"

Miss Estelee stood, but turned toward Frannie. "I'll leave you to think on that a spell. While you're thinking, you might want to consider your sister. She never let fear stand in her way, and for her, everything worked out just as it should."

With that, Miss Estelee walked away, singing as she crossed Town Square to the sidewalk on the less damaged side of town. *"Blessed assurance, Jesus is mine, Oh what a foretaste of glory divine . . ."*

"Frannie, thank goodness." Candi and her Aunt Verdi, Frannie's assistant, walked up to where she sat on the park bench. "We've been looking for you all day. We were so worried." Candi sat, and before Frannie knew what was happening, found herself in her friend's warm embrace. "I'm so glad you're here."

Verdi sat on the other side of Frannie, patting her arm. "When we saw your house, we were afraid you might have left town."

After Candi released her, Frannie looked at the two women she'd been closest to since coming to Angel Ridge. "I thought about it," she admitted.

"Well, we won't hear of it," Verdi said. "So just wipe those thoughts right out of your mind. Bill and I have been working all day. Our place doesn't have any damage, and we have a little older house on our property. Now, it's not much, but it's clean, and it has a nice bed, a bathroom, and a little kitchen. You'll find everything you need there to be comfortable until your house can be rebuilt."

Candi jumped in with, "And I've picked out enough clothes from my shop to tide you over until we can go into town to buy more. I've also got all the toiletries you might need packed up and moved over to your new little home."

Shocked, Frannie said, "I couldn't possibly —"

"Don't think to argue with us. It's done," Verdi insisted with a decisive nod.

"And I know your office is gone, but you can have the big room above my shop. I've never used it for anything but storage and a yoga space."

"We can start setting everything up tomorrow," Verdi said. "I backed up all the files to an Internet storage site, so we haven't lost any of our work."

"But how can we move forward with the Foundation when the buildings that would house the work are destroyed?"

"I'd say we need the Foundation now

more than ever," Verdi said. "It may not be your original vision, but we can still do job training in the space Candi is letting us use, and those people can still go to work with those businesses in town that volunteered to be part of the program. Most importantly, the town needs those workers to help us rebuild. Why, your Foundation could be pivotal to the town's recovery."

"But only if you'll agree to stay and lead the program," Candi said.

Frannie had started the Foundation because she'd wanted to make a difference in people's lives. She'd never imagined, at the same time, that the people working in the program could make a difference in other people's lives. Frannie smiled ruefully. She'd thought being happy in her work would bring her contentment, but true contentment came through forming meaningful relationships. Here in Angel Ridge, she could have both. Miss Estelee was right. All her dreams, plus all the happiness she'd never dared imagine, were within her grasp. All she had to do was reach out and take it.

Patrick left the hospital in the middle of the afternoon, promising Abby he'd be back that evening. He felt comfortable leaving her since the doctor had assured him that the surgery had gone well, and that she should sleep most of the next twenty-four hours. And besides that, Dixie was here. When he'd told her about Frannie disappearing while he'd slept, and also about the loss of her house, Dixie had promised to stay with Abby so he could go find Frannie to make sure she was okay.

Everything in town appeared to have been handled quite ably by the ones he'd left in charge, allowing him to scour the downtown area searching for Frannie. He asked everyone, including Mr. DeFoe — who knew just about as much as Dixie when it came to town happenings — if they'd seen her, but no one had. Finally, he'd run into Reverend Reynolds who told him about Frannie's encounter with Harriet McKay. Patrick could have happily walked into the bank and throttled Mrs. McKay, but his priority was finding Frannie.

"So, you just left her here alone after that?" Patrick asked.

"No. She sat here on the park bench speaking with Miss Estelee for some time. As they talked, I saw the color return to her face, and she seemed much improved when Miss Estelee left. Then Candi and Verdi came up to speak with her. After they talked, she got up and walked away."

"Which way did she go?" Patrick asked.

"Toward the diner."

"Thanks," Patrick said, then hurried over to the diner. When he pulled on the front door, it didn't budge. With Dixie out of town and no power available for cooking, the place was locked up. He turned and raked a hand through his hair. Where could she be?

The Tall Pines. Maybe she'd gone up there to think. He jogged all the way up the road leading to the clearing at the top of the hill. Scanning the open area, he didn't see anyone, so he called out. "Frannie? Are you here?"

Nothing. Bending down with his hands on his knees trying to catch his breath, a fear overtook him. What if she'd listened to Mrs. McKay's venom and left town? He couldn't let Frannie leave believing that no one wanted her in Angel Ridge. He had to find her and let her know — what? That he needed her? He'd told her that already, and apparently, it hadn't been enough for her to stay.

He turned and jogged back down the hill and all the way to his house. Without giving it much thought, he got in his car and began driving the roads that fanned out into the area just outside of town. If he'd been thinking clearly, he would have known that to be a waste of time. Why would she be out late in the afternoon, with darkness nearing, walking the roads?

But still he drove, until he found himself parked in front of the bar where they'd first met. Sitting in his car looking at the low, block, windowless building nudged that old familiar craving back to life. He could imagine the feel of the glass in his hand, the smell of the liquor, the taste of it on his tongue, the burn in his throat, and the numbing that would follow. Patrick squeezed his eyes shut against the longing to sink into that numbness and never emerge.

A knock on his window shocked his eyes opened, his head swinging to see who stood outside his car. A graying thin man he didn't recognize peered in the window at him. Patrick pressed the button to lower it.

"I'm glad you came along, mister. I need a ride into town. A tree fell on my car, and I need to see the Doc because I take insulin. I used the last of it this morning. I'm afraid I ain't able to walk all that way, and I can't call nobody with the phones out."

Patrick blinked, trying to focus on what the man was saying. "I'm sorry. What did you say your name was? I don't —"

"It's John. John Smith."

"You must be new —" Patrick never finished his sentence, because the man standing next to his car collapsed.

Frannie stood in the waiting area of Dr. Ferguson's office, so weak with relief that she had to grab the reception desk to keep from sliding to the floor.

Janice grasped her arm. "Here now, are you all right?"

Frannie pressed a hand to her chest. "Yes, just relieved that you got the tests back already and everything is fine." This day had been filled with everything — despair, then hope, and now joy.

"Well, I wouldn't call an overactive thyroid nothing. We'll need to monitor you closely. And it may take several medication adjustments before you see good results."

"Of course, but that's so much better than you telling me the cancer was back," Frannie insisted, giddy in her happiness. She stuffed the bag of medicines Janice had given her into a tote she'd gotten from Candi. "Thank you so much, Janice."

"My pleasure," Janice said. "In all the sadness and devastation of this day, I'm glad to be able to give you good news."

"Doc — Frannie!" Patrick burst through

the door, out of breath.

"Is something wrong, Patrick?" Janice said.

Frannie devoured Patrick with her eyes. He looked terrible and wonderful at the same time.

His gaze skidded to Frannie, then back to Janice. "There's an unconscious man in my car. I picked him up outside of town. He said he needed to come see you because he'd run out of insulin, and then he just collapsed."

Janice moved toward the door with Patrick, Frannie following close behind. "What's his name?" Janice asked.

"He said it was John Smith. He must be new in town, because I didn't recognize him at all."

"That name doesn't sound familiar, but no matter. Where did you say he was?"

"The backseat of my car."

Janice opened the backdoor of Patrick's sedan, both peered in, but no one was there. Patrick straightened and looked up and down the street. "He must have come to and wandered off."

"What did he look like?" Janice asked.

"Tall, thin, sixties, I'd say. Straight, long-ish gray hair."

"Let's split up," Janice suggested.

Patrick went one way, Janice the other, while Frannie searched around the doctor's house. When they met back at Patrick's car ten minutes later, no one had seen the man.

"Where could he have gone?" Patrick asked.

Janice shook her head. "I can't remember seeing anyone that meets that description before. Why don't we all go inside while I try and find a file on him?" As they walked back toward the house, Janice said, "Patrick, if you have a cell with service, call Grady and give him the man's description in case he shows up in town disoriented. Tell him if he sees the guy to get him to my office right away."

Patrick made the call, and Janice disappeared into the back of the house while Frannie just stared at Patrick. She wanted nothing more than the feel of his arms around her while she told him everything that had happened today, but she knew she had other things she needed to tell him first.

After making the call, Patrick turned to her. "Where have you been? You left the hospital without a word. I've been looking all over for you." He walked over to her, grasping her upper arms while he looked her over as if assuring himself she was all right. "I was worried sick," he admitted.

"I'm sorry. I — I couldn't stay there."

"Stay where? The hospital?"

Frannie nodded.

"It's just as I thought," Janice said. "No file on any John Smith."

"John Smith's made an appearance?" An older man with white hair and a snowy white beard, who looked remarkably like Santa, walked through the front door and straight to Janice's side. He leaned down to kiss her cheek.

"Hello, Uncle. How are the folks outside of town faring?"

"Everyone's fine, except there's no power, and of course, they wouldn't hear of coming to the shelter. Made of sterner stuff than that, and all. You know how mountain folk can be." Looking at Patrick and Frannie, the man said, "Patrick, how's our Abby?"

"Recovering from surgery, but doing well. They had to remove her spleen. One of her broken ribs punctured it."

"I'm sorry to hear that, but I'm certain she's receiving the finest medical treatment available if Janice here had anything to say about it, and I happen to know she did." He smiled lovingly at his grandniece.

Turning back to Patrick and Frannie, he said, "I don't believe I've had the pleasure."

"Sorry, Doc," Patrick said. "This is Frannie Thompson. Frannie, this is Doc Prescott. He's our recently retired town doctor."

"Ah, yes, our new town entrepreneur. I'm so sorry I missed the meeting last night. I've been up at my cabin on Laurel Mountain."

"I'm pleased to meet you," Frannie said.

"Likewise. Now, what's this I hear about John Smith?"

"Do you know him, Uncle?" Janice asked.

The older man tugged on his ear. "I wouldn't go that far, but he has been known to show up in town from time to time. Now, who says they saw him?"

"I did," Patrick said. "He came up to my car, knocked on my window and said he needed to get to the doctor because he'd run out of insulin."

"*Uh-huh, uh-huh.* And where was this?"

Patrick hesitated, not wanting to tell everyone he'd wound up at a bar when he wasn't sure himself how or why he'd gone there. "It was out off of Old Highway 32."

"There was some crisis out that way, was there?"

A crisis, indeed, Patrick thought. "The man said he didn't have a phone to call anyone, and then he passed out. I got him into my car and brought him here, then came in to get Janice. But when we got back to the car —"

"Don't tell me," Doc Prescott said, holding up a hand. "He wasn't there."

"Right. How did you know?" Janice asked.

"Well now, would you like to hear what I think or what Miss Estelee says?"

"Oh boy," Janice said. "I think I might want to hear both."

"Miss Estelee says he's a guardian angel."

"An angel," Patrick said flatly. "As in one of the angels she says watches over the town?"

"The same," Doc Prescott confirmed. "That's why I asked if there was an emergency out the way you found him."

Chills raced up and down Patrick's spine. He'd been sitting in his car, contemplating taking a drink and losing his sobriety, when the man had appeared. Could he have been an angel sent to save Patrick from himself?

"What do you think?" Janice asked her uncle.

"I think there are some things that simply cannot be explained. Like that little kitten that kept finding its way over here from Blake's house, at the other end of the road, when the two of you were courting."

"That's my house with Blake now," Janice smiled fondly at her uncle.

"And thankfully, the cat stays put with you."

"He's allergic," Janice explained.

"Well," Patrick said, "I called Grady and asked him to keep an eye out for the man. He's bound to show up."

"Not likely," Doc Prescott said, "but I'm happy to be proven wrong."

Patrick turned to Frannie. "Can I have a word with you?" he asked.

"Yes," she agreed. Looking back to Janice, she said, "Thank you again."

"Anytime," Janice said, seeing them to the door.

Patrick walked with Frannie off the porch and down the steps to the sidewalk. "Are you all right?" he asked.

"I'm fine," Frannie said. "But there's something I need to tell you. Can we go somewhere and talk?"

"Sure. Sammy's with my mom. We could go to my house."

"Oh, I'm sorry. Do you need to go pick him up?"

"No. I'm heading back to the hospital after I get a shower and change of clothes."

"I don't want to keep you, then. We can talk later," Frannie said.

"No, I want to talk to you, too." He opened the passenger door of his car for her and then drove them the short distance to his house. When he glanced over at her, he couldn't help noticing that she hadn't taken her eyes off him and that she looked . . . happier. "Are you sure you're okay?" he repeated.

"I'm great," she confirmed.

Great. The woman had just lost everything. He pulled up in front of his house, and they got out of the car. As they walked up to his front porch, with Frannie still giving him that intense look, Patrick asked, "Do you want to go inside or sit on the porch?"

Seeing the vacant space where her house had once stood, Frannie said, "Inside."

With no electricity, the sitting room at the front of Patrick's house was a bit stuffy. Frannie sat while he opened a couple of windows.

"Would you like a glass of water?" he asked.

"No." She patted the space on the sofa next to her. "Sit."

After he'd joined her, she put her hand in his and said, "I'm sorry I worried you today. You have enough on your mind without adding me going missing to your trouble."

He laced his fingers with hers. "You're no trouble to me." Frannie's face all but glowed. Everything about her seemed lighter. He couldn't resist touching her, so he reached out and ran a hand up and down her arm. "There's so much I want to say to you."

"And I want to hear it," Frannie said. "But first, I have to tell you something . . . that I've been keeping from you."

Patrick pulled back a bit, peering at her in the dim light. "That sounds serious."

"It is." Frannie closed her eyes, took a breath, then opened them, staring at their linked hands. Then, she decided to just get it over with. She raised her eyes to his and said, "Patrick, I'm —" Forming the words was harder than she'd imagined, especially given the scare she'd had today. She took another breath and continued. "I'm a cancer survivor."

CHAPTER 15

"I know I should have told you, given what you went through with Susan, but I didn't want anyone to know. When I moved to Angel Ridge, I just needed a fresh start where nobody knew that about me, that I'd been sick.

"But then, you were there and asking for so much from me, and you wouldn't take 'no' for an answer. But I convinced myself it didn't matter, because I wasn't going to let anything happen between us."

"That's why you told me the only relationship you'd consider was a physical one."

"One of the reasons. The truth is, I don't have a lot of experience with relationships. I didn't date growing up, because at the age most girls are going on their first dates, I'd lost my hair and had several rounds of chemotherapy." She pulled the band from her ponytail so she could feel her hair against her neck, just to reassure herself that it was still there. "Then as an adult, I settled into being alone because I always believed I wouldn't live to be old. I thought it would be selfish of me to want a husband when I knew how it would hurt him when I died. I didn't have close friends for the same reason."

Patrick looked like her words had physically struck him. "What about children?" he asked.

Frannie just shook her head. "I never considered them."

"Okay. So, are you saying you're in remission? That it will come back?"

"No. The doctors told me I'm completely cured, and that, with the type of cancer I had, recurrence is extremely rare. But when all you can remember is illness, hospitals, doctors, nurses and needles, your outlook can become fatalistic, or at least that's what the therapist told me."

"You had cancer as a child?"

Frannie nodded. "Leukemia."

"But you're well now?"

"Yes. I have to take medications and have regular checkups, but other than that, I'm fine."

"How long has it been since you were in treatment?"

"I was nineteen when I had my last chemo

treatment and twenty when the doctors released me."

Patrick stood and walked a few paces away. "I guess I see why you didn't tell me, but still, I wish I'd known."

"I understand." She focused on her hands in her lap. "I'm telling you now because, with the tornado, I've been looking at things differently. I mean, I could have died last night, but I didn't. I easily could have been in my house or my office when the tornado hit, but I wasn't. If I was going to die young, that would have been the perfect opportunity. But I'm still here. I wasn't even hurt."

Standing, Frannie walked over to Patrick. "Since I got sick, I've lived my life in fear, but Miss Estelee and Candi have helped me see that's not really living. None of us is promised tomorrow. It isn't just cancer that takes people from our lives. Cancer just gives us notice for a long goodbye. Tornados, car wrecks, heart attacks, explosions." She smiled, and then continued. "Any number of things can take us without warning."

She reached out and touched his arm, and Patrick felt himself leaning toward her until his hand snaked around her waist, pulling her up against his chest, next to his heart where she belonged.

"I don't want to waste another minute worrying about what might happen," she said.

"What are you saying?" Patrick asked softly.

Frannie touched his face, then trailed her hand down to his neck and back up into his hair. "I was considering giving in to you," she said just as softly. "That is, if you can accept this as part of what's made me who I am." When he didn't immediately respond, she added, "I understand if you can't. I know this is asking a lot, and that you might even need some time to consider."

He touched his forehead to hers and closed his eyes. Inhaling her sweet, floral scent, feeling her body against his, he began to fall into her. "It's a lot to take in. Imagining you sick, like Susan, for months and months, and then —"

Frannie pressed her lips to his, stopping his words. "I'm healthy. There's no reason to believe I'll get sick again." She trailed her fingers along his jaw, then lifted her lips to his again in a soft, warm, comforting caress. God, he needed this woman like he needed to breathe.

Breaking the contact, she said, "Still, you have a lot of things that will demand your time and attention, not just now, but for months to come."

"And you have a home and a business to rebuild." He leaned back, so he could see her expression. "You are staying."

"I want to."

"Why do I sense a 'but' in that statement?"

Shaking her head and laughing, Frannie said, "Because this morning, I was certain that I should leave Angel Ridge, and now I just said out loud that I want to stay. It's crazy. My physical home and the buildings that housed my business are gone, but those places weren't really my home or my business."

Patrick shook his head. "You lost me."

"It's the people that make a home, and it turns out, they make the business, too. Candi and Verdi convinced me that I can keep the business going with the people participating helping to rebuild the town. Verdi has a small house on her farm where I can live, and Candi is giving me the space above Heart's Desire to use as my temporary office."

"Sounds perfect." *Except that he'd rather have her staying with him.* A shadow passed across Frannie's face that had her pressing against his chest and stepping back out of his arms. Patrick didn't want to let her go.

314

"Perfect except for this thing between us. It's so complicated, and neither of us is going to have a lot of time for," she shifted a hand back and forth between them, "seeing what this can become."

"True," Patrick agreed, taking a step toward her, closing the gap between them. "But if we work through all those things together . . ." He took her hand, lacing their fingers together, and pulled her back to the couch. After he sat, he pulled her down beside him, his arms around her. "Abby likes you. I think you might be able to give her some support in the coming months." He pressed a kiss on that place behind her ear that he loved so much. "Sammy likes you." He trailed his lips down the side of her neck, liking the way she shivered. "And I like you."

She sighed. "I like you, too."

"And I don't come without baggage. I'm an alcoholic."

"But you're sober."

Time for more honesty. "This afternoon, after I'd scoured the town looking for you, I got a little crazy. When I couldn't find you, I wound up at the bar where we met, not knowing how I got there. If it hadn't been for that man collapsing and needing to get to the doctor, I might have gone in for a drink."

"I don't believe that. Just because you thought about having a drink doesn't mean you would have done it."

"I'm not so sure."

"I am."

Patrick touched her face. "I like that you believe in me." He felt so much stronger just hearing those words from her.

"Maybe that man was a guardian angel, just like Doc Prescott said."

Leaning in, he kissed her cheek and said, "I think you're my angel."

Smiling, she teased his lips with a soft kiss that ended too soon. "I'm not an angel."

He buried his hand in her hair. "*Mmm . . .* I like the sound of that."

"So, you really think we'd make a good team?" She breathed the words across his lips.

He pressed his lips to hers. "I'd like to try. What do you say?"

Staring at him for long moments, she asked, "Are you sure?"

"Are you?" he countered.

She leaned back, playing with a button on his shirt. "I think we should take it slow." Raising her beautiful eyes to his, she continued. "A relationship between us could be difficult for your children, and you need to really think about how you feel about my having had cancer."

"Would you mind if I talk to Janice about that?"

"No, of course not. We could talk to her together, that way we can both answer any questions you have."

He took her hands and held them in his, considering. "As much as the thought of you having cancer terrifies me, the thought of not having you in my life doesn't even bear considering. If I'd known how it would all turn out, that Susan would die young, I wouldn't have changed having her in my life or having her as the mother of our children. Even though our relationship wasn't a passionate one, we had love and laughter and two wonderful children together." He brought her hands to his lips. "What I'm trying to say is that I've never felt this way for anyone, Frannie. I don't know what the future holds, but I know I want you in my life because I'm in love with you."

Frannie felt her heart turn over in her chest. "I love you, too," she said.

And then, words ended so they could express their feelings another way. The kiss they shared formed an unspoken bond between them. It also held the promise of a future filled with an unforgettable love and passion they would share together.

DIXIE'S FAREWELL

With a little help from her friends

"Hey, y'all. Come on in and join us. The ladies of Angel Ridge decided, given the insanity of the past few months, that we'd gather in the 'tea' room at Heart's Desire to put our feet up and enjoy each other's company along with a couple of bottles of wine, or three."

Dixie lifted a glass. "Here's to surviving and loving in Angel Ridge."

"Yes, where do things stand with you and that delicious Jonathan Temple?" Janice Thornton Ferguson, Dixie's sister-in-law asked.

"Don't let my brother hear you speaking of his best friend in those terms," Dixie warned.

Ignoring that, Janice raised her eyebrows in question.

"Things between Jonathan and me are not

standing, sitting, or otherwise. I can't go there," Dixie said flatly.

"But you want to," Candi Heart supplied.

"Who wouldn't?" added Josie Allen Craig, the town librarian.

All the women burst into laughter and clinked glasses.

"Shocking. What would your husband say?" Dixie asked.

"Cole knows he has nothing to worry about, but that does not mean that I'm blind, and that Jonathan Temple is a fine specimen of a man."

"He's so big and strong," Candi said.

"Makes a girl wonder if all of him is big," Josie added.

"And strong," Candi added.

"Ladies!" Dixie said, but her complaint was drowned out by laughter and more clinking of glasses.

"Maybe Janice can tell us," Candi suggested.

"Sorry. Doctor-patient privilege."

"So professional," Josie complained.

"Speaking of handsome, strong men," Janice said, "Candi, how are the wedding plans going? I hope the storm hasn't delayed things."

"We were going to get married in Town Square, but with the town in such a state of rebuilding, we decided to move the ceremony up to the Tall Pines."

"That's where Blake and I got married," Janice said. "It's a magical spot for a wedding."

"Grady has been a patient man," Dixie said. "How long have the two of you been engaged?"

"Long enough," Candi said, laughing.

"And speaking of patience, could we soon hear more wedding bells ring in Angel Ridge, Frannie?"

Frannie sipped her wine, oblivious to the conversation.

"Earth to Frannie," Dixie said, snapping her fingers.

"What?" Frannie blinked, now giving her attention to Dixie. "I'm sorry. What?"

"I know that dreamy look," Janice said. "She's thinking, finally, a night off, and I'm out with the girls instead of a certain mayor of this fair town."

"Sorry," Frannie smiled, ducking her head as a blush colored her cheeks and neck.

"Don't apologize. We all know that particular feeling," Josie said. "The men of this town certainly know how to put a smile on a woman's face."

"Thank you, Jesus. I'll drink to that," Janice said, lifting her glass.

Everyone joined in except for Dixie. "Y'all didn't grow up with them."

"Oh, deny it all you want," Candi said, "but I predict that you'll have that same smile on your face by the end of the year. From what I can see, Jonathan is willing to do whatever it takes to win you back."

"Have you been gazing into that crystal ball, or whatever it is you use to see the future?" Dixie asked.

"The way he looks at you and the way you insist you have no feelings for him, it doesn't take any special powers to see that the two of you are crazy in love."

"Sometimes love isn't enough," Dixie said.

"Love," Frannie said, "is all that matters." She reached across the table and took Dixie's hand. "Don't let past troubles steal your chance at happiness. Patrick and I have had so much to overcome, but by focusing on what was right in front of us, all of that faded away. I'm so glad we gave ourselves the gift of a chance for happiness firmly planted in the present."

"You're lucky, Frannie," Candi said. "It takes most people a lifetime to gain that kind of wisdom."

Dixie pulled her hand out of Frannie's and poured herself another glass of wine. "Well, I never claimed to be wise. All I know is that I can't trust him. Don't get me wrong, I'm simply thrilled that all of y'all have found your happily ever afters. It just wasn't meant to be for me and Jonathan."

"Or maybe the last chapter of that story has yet to be written," Candi said.

"Anyway," Dixie said, "it's time for us to bid our guests goodbye so we can get on with our girl's night. I'm hoping Candi can be persuaded to break out some of her blackberry moonshine."

"I just happen to have some in my work-room," Candi said, as she rose to go get it.

"We sure are glad y'all chose to visit with us in Angel Ridge. When you come back, we hope to have all this mess from the storm cleaned up. In Angel Ridge, we might not agree on everything, but we pull together in a crisis, just as we have in this one. Even Mrs. McKay has warmed to Frannie's job training program, now that she's seen how much help the folks involved have been in rebuilding. Why, they've cared for our town as if it were their own home. And who knows, maybe it will become their home. All I know is we've been blessed by these new additions to our town.

"Frannie came to Angel Ridge just a few months ago, but in the short time she's been here, she's shown us that outsiders do have a place among us. She's been an angel, not only to this town, but also to Patrick and his family, who can finally heal from the tragedies that have marked their pasts.

"So, come on back and see us again real soon. Who knows, maybe next June, we'll be hosting more than one wedding."

ACKNOWLEDGEMENTS

Janene Cates Putman, friend and publicity guru, thank you for your invaluable input on this project and on all the other Angel Ridge Novels.

I couldn't do this without you.

I'm glad I won't ever have to!

DIXIE'S READER'S GUIDE

1. One of the themes of "Unforgettable" is that of being present in the now. How did you see this theme being played out in the book? How does this theme play out in your own life?

2. Frannie's and Patrick's fears initially kept them from having a real relationship. What were their fears and how did they affect each of them? What are your fears? What effect do they have on your life? I, myself, am fearless, but what would you do if you were fearless?

3. Personally, I say, "Live and let live," and "The greater the risk, the bigger the payoff." Are you more like Patrick — with his inability to forgive himself and get past his guilt — or more like Frannie — with her playing it safe and doing what was expected of her? In what ways and why?

4. Patrick can always count on Dixie to give him hell. Do you have a "Dixie" in your life to tell it like it is? If so, how does that help you? If not, who could play that role for you?

5. Candi "just knows things" and told Frannie that can be a gift and a curse. In what aspect of your personality do you feel this? For me, it's my ability to spin conspiracy theories — like Frank Sinatra having Marilyn Monroe killed and the royal family getting rid of Princess Di. What would it take for you, like Candi, to accept it as a part of you?

6. Both Dixie and Frannie noted that one's actions demonstrate one's character. In both cases, these actions were in the past. Do you tend to judge others on their past? More importantly, do you tend to judge yourself based on your past? How can you move past that and live in the now?

7. Frannie wanted to make a difference in the lives of others. How did she live out that passion? With my cooking, I change lives daily. What is your passion? What are you doing about it today?

8. Frannie thought Patrick would be crazy

to get involved with a cancer survivor. Susan, Patrick and Jonathan wanted to hide the truth from Dixie to keep her from getting hurt. I have my own strong opinion on this, but what do you think? Were these decisions good or bad? Well-meaning or selfish? Do you make or have you made decisions to "protect" others? What was the result?

9. Mrs. McKay (visualize me turning my head and spitting here) was adamant that the storm and its resulting destruction were a sign that Frannie and her Foundation should not be in Angel Ridge. Do you believe in signs? Describe a time in your life that you were seemingly given a sign — did you misinterpret it or was it something you should have seen in a different light?

10. Miss Estelee said, "It's a beautiful day to be alive and livin' on the Ridge, ain't it?" How do your surroundings affect your mood? your activity? your productivity?

11. I love me a big, strong, silent man. What is the significance of Angel Ridge's angel monument? How is it important that it was the only thing untouched during the storm?

12. Candi said, "Right here in this moment

is where we were meant to be. Our only job is to live in the now of our lives." Agree or disagree? Is this a concept you would like to integrate into your own life?

ABOUT THE AUTHOR

Deborah Grace Staley is a life-long resident of East Tennessee. Married to her college sweetheart, she lives in the foothills of the Smoky Mountains in a circa 1867 farmhouse that has angel's wings in the gingerbread trim. In addition to being an award winning and Amazon bestselling author, in her spare time, Deborah enjoys spending time with her family and recently received a Master of Fine Arts degree in Creative Writing from Goddard College in Port Townsend, Washington. She now writes full-time and teaches. Deborah loves to hear from readers. Please contact her at: P.O. Box 672, Vonore, TN 37885 or via her website at deborahgracestaley.com.

The employees of Thorndike Press hope you have enjoyed this Large Print book. All our Thorndike, Wheeler, and Kennebec Large Print titles are designed for easy reading, and all our books are made to last. Other Thorndike Press Large Print books are available at your library, through selected bookstores, or directly from us.

For information about titles, please call:
(800) 223-1244

or visit our Web site at:
http://gale.cengage.com/thorndike

To share your comments, please write:
Publisher
Thorndike Press
10 Water St., Suite 310
Waterville, ME 04901